NOT THE SAME ROAD OUT

Not the Same Road Out

Trans Canada Stories

Edited by
K.J. Denny

TIDEWATER
PRESS

Copyright © 2025 K.J. Denny (editor)

All rights reserved. No part of this publication may be reproduced, stored in a retrieval system or transmitted in any form or by any means—electronic, mechanical, audio recording, or otherwise—without the written permission of the publisher.

Published by Tidewater Press
New Westminster, BC, Canada
tidewaterpress.ca

978-1-990160-50-9 (print)
978-1-990160-51-6 (e-book)

"The Road In Is Not the Same Road Out" first published in *Poetry London*, Autumn 2012, Issue 73
Back cover map courtesy of Trans Canada Trail, tctrail.ca

LIBRARY AND ARCHIVES CANADA CATALOGUING IN PUBLICATION
Title: Not the same road out : Trans Canada stories / edited by K.J. Denny.
Names: Denny, K. J., editor.
Identifiers: Canadiana (print) 20250204428 | Canadiana (ebook) 20250205947 | ISBN 9781990160509 (softcover) | ISBN 9781990160516 (EPUB)
Subjects: LCSH: Trans Canada Trail—Fiction. | CSH: Short stories, Canadian (English) | CSH: Canadian fiction (English)—21st century. | LCGFT: Short stories.
Classification: LCC PS8329.1 .N68 2025 | DDC C813/.0108327109052—dc23

Canadä

Tidewater Press gratefully acknowledges the support of the Government of Canada.

PRINTED IN CANADA

To the trailways of Canada and all who travel them.

Contents

The Road In Is Not the Same Road Out KAREN SOLIE	ix
Field Notes on Cryptids (Ontario) ANNE BALDO	1
Invasive Species (Northwest Territories) LILLIAN AU	21
Red Shoes in the Dust (Alberta) TERRY WATADA	37
Eirenopolis (Manitoba) SEYWARD GOODHAND	49
Kick-Ass (Prince Edward Island) LAUREN LAFRANCE	61
Adrift (New Brunswick) BEV VINCENT	75
Roadside Reunion (British Columbia) BILL ENGLESON	90
So Late in the Season (Nova Scotia) TRICIA SNELL	103
Movie Night (Newfoundland and Labrador) TRACY KREUZBURG	124
The Light in the Sky (Quebec) SHARON HUNT	134
Soldiers Summit (Yukon) MATTHEW HENEGHAN	157
Static (Saskatchewan) DEE HOBSBAWN-SMITH	167
The Boat (Nunavut) PATRICK WOODCOCK	175
Contributors	190

The Road In Is Not the Same Road Out

KAREN SOLIE

The perspective is unfamiliar.
We hadn't looked back going in,
and lingered too long
at the viewpoint. It was a prime-of-life
experience. Many things we know
by their effects: void in the rock
that the river may advance, void
in the river that the fish may advance,
helicopter in the canyon
like a fly in a jar, a mote in the eye,
a wandering cause. It grew dark,
a shift change and a shift
in protocol. To the surface of the road
a trail rose, then a path to the surface
of the trail. The desert
sent its loose rock up to see.
An inaudible catastrophic orchestra
is tuning, we feel it in the air
driven before it, as a pressure
on the brain. In the day
separate rays fall so thickly
from their source we cannot perceive
the gaps between them. But night

NOT THE SAME ROAD OUT

is absolute, uniform and self-
derived, the formerly irrelevant
brought to bear, the progress
of its native creatures unimpeded.
We have a plan between us, and then we
have our own. Land of the five
corners, the silent partner, 500 dollars
down, no questions, the rental car
stops at the highway intersection, a filthy
violent storm under the hood. It yields
to traffic from both directions.
It appears it could go either way.

Field Notes on Cryptids

ANNE BALDO

Ontario | Friendship Trail

The fourth time I ask Finley about the punctuation in Letizia's texts, specifically the double exclamation marks (*I love it! That sounds so fun!!*), he says, "Nattie, why are you so obsessed with her?" We are in the car, on the way to meet up with Letizia, and Arlo. We've only been driving an hour. "I didn't know you still even talked to her anymore." And for almost twenty years, we hadn't. Not until Letizia saw the hunter's photograph of a Bigfoot by Elliot Lake, crossing the Coureurs de Bois section of the Voyageur Trail, just past Spine Road.

Nattie, this reminded me of you, and a link to the article. At the end: *I miss you*.

I say, "I don't think I'm obsessed. I'm just trying to figure out if you think she's being sincere about our new logo project or if she's like, making fun of us?"

Ten years after working for a lice removal service, Finley had recently started his own. I thought the name, Lice Savers, was ambiguous, but Finley was enthusiastic. Together we'd created a logo, a louse in a red circle, slashed. A little too *Ghostbusters*, but still.

Finley leans over, switches the radio station. "Who cares if she is?"

But I was like that, holding onto everything. Things didn't so much live rent-free in my head as squat there, destroying the place.

We should get together sometime, Letizia had written. When I read the message, I had to put my phone down. Pace the house, deep breathing the way I'd worked on in therapy, four sessions before I quit. The therapist, Lana, wore huge earrings shaped like gold leopards and asked me if I'd ever considered looking on the bright side.

I made myself wait an hour to reply to Letizia. *Yeah, I'd like that.* Hoping to come off as cool, devoid of anxiety. Knew I had to slow it down. Like so many times before, trying to blunt my desire.

Arlo and I are going to stay a week in Port Colbourne if you and Finley want to meet us –

"Are you going to be like this the whole trip?" Finley glances at me. "Because maybe it's a bad idea."

Since we'd been married, Finley and I had never gone anywhere. Not like Letizia and Arlo, her Instagram of sepia sunsets on Shale Beach, the Cavendish Dunelands, the Tulip Festival in Ottawa. Once a year, my parents or his took Amelia and Daisy, our daughters, and we stayed at the casino in downtown Windsor, twelve minutes from home. Out, we'd talk about the girls, how the casino restaurants used to be better, the time we won two hundred dollars, then fall asleep early, the hotel room lit by the muted glow of *Law & Order* reruns. Always back home the next day by ten at the latest. And now we were going to the Clifftop House, a cottage by the Friendship Trail, surrounded by birch trees, sugar maples. A view of Lake Erie. Letizia sent me photos. The Welland Canal, a hummingbird dipping into pink bee balm, whimsical cottage art—suncatchers in trees, windchimes, a broken glass mosaic garden path winding between wintercreeper and juniper.

I bet it will feel like twenty years never passed, Letizia had said.

Arlo was the only boy in our Cryptids and Philosophy course, a small class, twelve of us. The low enrolment surprised me. Because what could be more interesting? Arlo told us he was only there for an easy credit, which I found secretly disappointing. He liked to wear ironic T-shirts or these newsboy caps and coordinating vests.

He dressed like an extra on *Peaky Blinders*, which wasn't a show back then, so I just thought he looked dapper and quirky. He had a mean, scoffing way of looking at the world, and the rest of us in the class, mostly still teenaged girls, hopscotched around him, affectionate and doting.

One day I wore my *Vertigo* T-shirt, James Stewart falling in a spiral over Madeleine's silhouette.

"Is that how you feel today?" he said.

"Dizzy?" I'd asked. "Or haunted by the ghost of a lost love and my personal failure?"

Arlo laughed, and we sat together after that, him and me and Letizia. Letizia taking notes assiduously as Arlo and I scratched messages back and forth to each other in the margins of our notebooks. *Should I dye my hair black?* I asked, and Arlo wrote, *Nattie, don't be emo.*

Did Mothman value goodness? What makes us human, and a creature like the Loveland Frog not? If we discovered the existence of Sasquatch, would they have legal rights like us? Would they have the same need for love that we as humans did? In my essay on the last subject, I argued yes. I got an A.

Letizia had not, like me, spent her childhood collecting cryptid clippings from newspapers in a photo album, but she took the class seriously, as she took all her classes seriously. Arlo, however, was not a true believer in either cryptids or academic diligence. By the time we wrote our final exams in May, we'd formed a trinity. "Is Arlo coming?" one of us would always ask the other when we went out. When it was only Letizia and me, we offered his opinion on things, what he would say about the movie we went to watch, or how cute it was he was learning to juggle. We were like parents who, finally out on a date alone, could not stop talking about our child.

At the cottage, I park in the gravel driveway, loose stones bordered by chokecherry, lacy with white flowers. In the months leading up to this, I'd obsessively checked my messages, and when I heard my cell's chime, my heart briefly glowed, hoping it was Letizia, the feeling not unlike when I'd first met Finley and the phone would ring.

She wrote *I still think of you*, and I parsed the meaning of each emoticon, which Letizia told me were not called emoticons anymore but were now called emojis. Stressed over my own, erred on the side of profusion—multiple hearts, rows of yellow smilies. Sometimes she would text me back after weeks—*I've been really bad at replying*—and I'd have to force myself to delay, to not answer moments later, disclosing my needy heart.

Some nights she'd swarm me with messages. She asked about the girls, and I told her about Daisy's sudden birth, my subsequent postpartum anxiety so bad I'd stay up all night after night. So exhausted shadows moved at the edge of my vision like quick birds I couldn't fully glimpse. I'd dump bottles of milk left out of my sight because, if I hadn't been watching, how could I say for certain an intruder hadn't come in, poisoned them? Letizia told me about her art, her jewellery business on Etsy, how she used only raw stones. How her birthstone cuff bracelet, created with recycled metals, had made the "Five Best Purchases Our Editors Made in February" list in *Chatelaine*. About what colour she was going to redo the walls of her living room, if white trim was the right choice. I'd go to bed soothed, thinking of Letizia's new pale lilac walls.

We traded poems we were reading, articles about talking to your houseplants or unsolved mysteries. We agreed we were finally processing our childhoods, our teen years toxic in ways we didn't understand or only accepted as normal back then. The constant tabloid covers featuring stars with cellulite, celebrities mocked in paparazzi beach shots, women who had the nerve to age, to wrinkle or thicken in any way. Conversely, the magazines ridiculed the girls who took it too far—fake concern for actresses with ribs visible beneath their slip dresses, with shoulder blades protruding. How you were not supposed to be either, and how impossible it was. Joan Rivers mocking Kate Winslet, saying she was the reason the *Titanic* sank. We'd study our own bodies in mirrors, in dressing rooms at the mall, like Kate's or bigger, possibly, and felt, down to our bones, how unacceptable we must be, how monstrous.

The flies buzz in the grass. A quartz crystal suncatcher shimmers from a birch branch. Finley and I wait on the porch. We ring the doorbell, and it sounds like birds.

"A cerulean warbler," Finley says.

The door opens. Letizia, bright white T-shirt slipped into a long skirt, big leafy green print. Layered gold necklaces, turquoise seed beads. "I'm so glad you made it. Arlo just stepped out to get groceries. He should be back any minute. He can't wait to explain his new therapeutic techniques to you."

"Should be great." When I'd mentioned Lana the therapist to Letizia, I hadn't expected she'd share that with Arlo, assuming it would fall under some confidential umbrella. But of course it didn't. Letizia was not paid to keep my secrets, like Lana was. Did I know Arlo had left his job in Human Resources, gone back to school, got a degree in social work, Letizia asked? No, I did not. And he was hoping to open his own practice, specializing in new methods of treating trauma and negative memories. He was looking for experience, Letizia said, and maybe I could give it a try, work through some of what she called my issues. When I looked over Arlo's Instagram profile, I saw he'd updated his bio: *Emotion Coach*. He posted about defeating overthinking, about healthy communication in relationships, and approximately a dozen photographs of unbelievably blue skies.

"Your room is the loft upstairs," Letizia says. "I hope you don't mind. Arlo can't sleep up there, you know, his fear of heights." Then she leans in, hugs me lightly, the tricky way you hold something easily damaged, an eggshell, a dried flower. "Oh, they found out

NOT THE SAME ROAD OUT

that Bigfoot they saw up by Spine Road was just a bear with mange, by the way."

"That's too bad," I say. I'd been hoping, the way I always did, that it had been real.

Before we met, Finley had been a hockey player. An enforcer, someone prized not for their skill on the ice but their readiness for violence. "Does blood really bounce on the ice?" I asked when I met him. We'd gone to the Applebee's at the outlet mall on Huron Line for our first date. He'd flipped his fake teeth out over chicken fingers, wrapped them in a napkin.

"That's a myth," Finley had said. And he would know. His lip split, teeth rattling like candy in a glass jar. His eyebrow riven where a puck had once hit him, crinkled with scar tissue. Once stitched, he'd went right back on the ice, finished the game.

There were some players you fought and some you wouldn't, and you were supposed to leave already injured ones alone. A code of honour, really, or there had been once, he said. The first shove. The dropped gloves. The jersey cuffed. In a way each clash was like two people in the moment right before they kissed. How you read their body language, leaned closer in and went for it, having faith you could take whatever blood and pain came from it.

"Are you okay?" Finley asks, when we are unpacking in the bedroom. I heap dresses in a drawer while Finley puts things away more carefully—his button-up shirts with the wrinkle-resistant finish, whatever athlete's biography he is reading this month, the lavender-scented lice repellent shampoo we use.

Down below, I hear Letizia washing dishes at the sink. I'm still recalculating this Letizia with my teenage Letizia—turquoise Aeropostale hoodies, layered tank tops, denim skirts, hoop earrings. She had emerged, like a mayfly, from awkward, gangly underwater nymph to this—a gauzy, winged being. Meanwhile, I'd cycled backwards, gone larval, sluggish and juvenile.

"Of course." Not wanting to say how uncomfortable it felt, how maybe Finley was right, and we shouldn't have come here. Because I didn't want to remember being a teenager, not those last years anyway, and now here with Letizia I was nineteen again. Platform sandals with the thick foam soles and the stiff strap that cut between your toes. White eyeshadow, our cropped cardigans. The promises we made on the gym treadmills, the way we smiled and fell in line for the double standards of boys. Journal entries bleeding with emo lyrics. The phone calls from guys we were sort of dating but not really that left us feeling lonely, knowing what they were—their loveless words the equivalent of putting the least amount of change possible in a parking meter, hoping you could hold your place, buy a little time. And that so many times it worked.

At nineteen, Letizia and I watched *Desperate Housewives* on the phone together every Sunday night. We went on walks and joked about how we would meet Nicolo Costa, an extraordinarily handsome personal injury lawyer smiling on billboards all over Windsor.

"Shove me on an icy sidewalk."

"Help me fake a slip and fall at the grocery store."

We stayed up till sunrise and said things like, "I'm in love with you," and it didn't feel untrue, only impossible, ultimately. On Halloween, we went out dressed in cat ears and lingerie, and Arlo rolled his eyes, "Oh, you're those kind of girls," but he came with us anyway and in the photos we leaned in close to take, we are all smiling. Nineteen years old, downtown in our best Charlotte Russe halter minidresses or else a going-out top from Siren's, silk and lace over jeans, back when the city seemed alive and exciting at night and not just exhausting.

One day we were at Arlo's house playing Jenga when Letizia smiled.

NOT THE SAME ROAD OUT

"Let's play strip Jenga," she said.

We took off our shoes, our socks, one by one. Arlo lost his shirt. But when we got down to it, sitting there barefoot in our jeans and T-shirts, and I had the hem of my shirt in my hands, ready to go, Letizia said we were done. Relieved, I slid my socks back on.

"Were you really going to do it?" Driving back home, Letizia didn't look at me, messing with the zipper of her cherry-print purse. Her nails newly painted frosty lavender, Moonbeam, her favourite shade.

"I don't know," I said. "Maybe."

"That would be kind of slutty, though," she said. "Don't you think?"

I should've known back then, from the night I called Letizia to ask if she wanted to meet for coffee and she said, 'I have to go. Arlo's taking me to see this Nirvana cover band at the Loop, Never Mind. He asked if you wanted to go but I thought you were working," even though we worked the same job, banquet servers at weddings, and we knew each other's shifts. "I think it's too late to buy tickets, Nattie, I'm sorry."

"You don't even like Nirvana."

"Well. You don't even like Arlo and you were ready to take your top off in his kitchen last week."

"It was only a game and it was your idea."

"Okay, whatever."

"What if I do," I said. "Like Arlo."

"No." Letizia hesitated. "You can't."

"Why not?"

Her voice flickering just a little. "Nattie, this isn't fair to Arlo. He's leaving when we graduate. He needs to start all over. Not with you, not with me, either. You have to let him go."

Back then, late nights, after classes were done for the day, or I'd got home from work, or home from wherever we'd been, Arlo and I would stay up for hours messaging each other.

You're like one of three people I can stand being around for extended periods of time, he typed. *You should feel special.* And I did. I'd sit at the computer on the desk in the chill of the air-conditioned living room, *Seinfeld* reruns on before *Letterman* as we talked about our professors and part-time jobs (*I'm going to wake up early and call in sick*) and the movies he loved, usually ones I said didn't go anywhere and Arlo would argue *you have to be patient.*

It was so late, the last time. The talk shows had ended and the infomercials and dating shows were on, slimy ones like *ElimiDate* that always ended up in a hot tub. Sometimes a woman got to choose but usually it was a man in the midst of four women. We'd watch it together, over messenger, making predictions on who would be cut, who'd last till the end.

Troy is totally going to elimidate Melissa.
Yeah, maybe.
Are you okay? You seem different. Well if you need something you know where I am.

Once I'd told Arlo how I'd been so afraid of vampires when I was a kid. I'd lined the windowsill with cloves of garlic, went to bed in turtlenecks, stayed up all night.

Lucky for you, Nattie, I have lifetime immunity from vampires.
Yeah?
I won it in a poker game in Transylvania.
Sounds fake.
Signed by the king of vampires himself.
Dracula? You can't trust him.
Just stick with me, Nat, he'd said. *You'll be safe.*

When I come down from the loft, they are already sitting, all three of them around the weathered table, walnut wood.

NOT THE SAME ROAD OUT

"We want people to start saying *all clear* instead of *all clean,*" Finley is explaining. "We want to eliminate the shame associated with lice."

Arlo nods. "That makes sense. Reduce the stigma."

"Exactly," Finley says.

Arlo, unlike Letizia, looks so much the same. Before, he'd worn thrift store T-shirts—souvenirs from obscure museums, defunct sports teams. Now, in a faded Montreal Expos crewneck sweater, he sits across from Finley, passing a bowl of an elegant salad—green endives, crimped purple radicchio. "Hello, Natalie."

We used to laugh at his jokes, even the mean ones. Once Letizia expressed her surprise about friends of ours who'd started dating, how incompatible they seemed, and he'd said, "Sometimes you have to sacrifice your ideals for guaranteed sex in your forties." Now I wonder not at the cynicism of the first part, but the optimism of the second. As if anything was ever guaranteed.

A mason jar of wildflowers, burlap placemats with hemmed edges. Letizia has removed her necklaces, changed into a linen dress that ties in the back, made from organic flax, I knew. She'd sent a picture before buying it, asking what shade—cloudy grey or cream? Now she smiles, glassily. "How's everything going at the daycare?"

When I told her years ago that that was what I was doing, going to college to study early childhood education, she gave a sad, scornful look. "Don't you think you could do better? I'd rather choose to focus on the arts. I hope you don't regret it."

"It's good," I say now. "I like it." Which was mostly true, most days, although sometimes—peeling chewed string cheese from its wrapper or icing another bite—I did wonder how it would have been, somewhere else.

"That's so nurturing of you. It must be so fulfilling. That's what Arlo says about his new career. About how he's helping people heal."

One time we'd tried to go out, the four of us. After Letizia and

Arlo had been together five months, at least, and I had just met Finley. For weeks, any plans with Letizia had fallen apart.

"Sorry I didn't call you last night, Nattie," Letizia had said, calling me the morning after Canada Day. "Arlo picked me up from work and then we went back to his house and whatever and by the time I realized it, the fireworks were over—"

"I don't like fireworks, anyway."

But that night we'd gone bowling, split into teams. Finley and I had won, our combined score over two hundred, and I'd seen it as a sign of our solid collaboration.

"Nattie cheated," Arlo said. "I saw her step over the line like a dozen times."

Bowling shoes already off, I stood there, feeling ridiculous in my socks. "I did not."

"Plus you were throwing the ball."

"It's called lofting," Finley said. "It's not against the rules. Professional bowlers do it."

And Arlo said, "Of course you'd stand up for her. But you don't need to defend her with me. I've been her friend longer than you've been —"

"So," I say to Arlo now, "are you still juggling?"

Arlo looks at me. "What are you talking about?"

"Like you used to."

"Natalie, that was twenty years ago," he says, and I feel unbelievably juvenile, as if I'd still expected him to be playing with Matchbox cars or Ninja Turtles.

Letizia drops fried squash blossoms onto her dish. "We were thinking after dinner, maybe you'd want to get started."

"There's some paperwork," Arlo says.

"It's been a long day." A flower wilts over my fork. "Maybe I should just go to bed. Get an early start tomorrow morning."

"That's a good idea," Arlo says. "You should be clearheaded."

NOT THE SAME ROAD OUT

"We can visit Cave Springs tomorrow." Letizia's plate is littered with limp petals. "I hope you brought good shoes."

I think of my new block-heel sandals, pale lilac. My heels had blistered so quickly I'd driven most of the way barefoot. "I didn't."

"You can borrow some of Arlo's, then."

I'd promised Arlo I'd come over and help with his project, a series of photographs illustrating a poem by Sharon Thesen for our Canadian Poetry class. He'd chosen "Loose Woman Poem," and asked me to wear a dress. "Like you go downtown in."

It felt strange to look like this in daylight. Stilettos, mascara, frosted white lip gloss, short strapless black dress.

"You look perfect," Arlo said, opening the door. Waiting, for a moment. "Come on in."

I followed him inside, down the stairs to his basement apartment. "How was the show last night with Letizia?"

"It was fine. They tried to play their own songs, but I mean there's a reason some bands are cover bands, you know? It was like just shut up and play 'Come as You Are.' Anyway. How was work?"

"I didn't have a shift."

"Really? I guess Letizia was wrong." Arlo picked up his camera from the coffee table we'd found by the roadside last summer. "First we'll take the picture for 'Next day 222's / & the moon falls out / of my fingernail.'"

"Sure."

The only pills in his apartment were expired Gravol. He opened the bottle, shook the contents out. I cupped the pills in my palm as he snapped a few photos, flicked through the shots on his digital camera.

"Okay," he said, handing me the cordless phone. "Let's go to the bathtub so we can take a picture for the lines about talking on the phone in the bath."

The bathroom in Arlo's apartment was a sunny remnant of the seventies—yellow countertop and ruined daisy wallpaper, marigold towels and an amber glass soap dish filled with cakey, pinkish seashell soap that left a greasy lather on your hands.

"So I was thinking you could stand in the bathtub," Arlo said, pushing back the floral vinyl shower curtain. Tentatively, I stepped over the edge in my heels. I'd straightened my hair but I could feel it snaking back already in the dampness. "It doesn't look real," he said. "The way you're holding the phone. Maybe you can say something."

"Like what?"

"Anything." Arlo climbed into the empty bathtub, beside me. "Just look like you're really having a conversation."

I cradled the phone to my ear, half-turned away, pulled a sticky strand of my hair from my glassy lip gloss, began talking. "I was with my mom this morning, telling her how I used to be terrified of being abducted by aliens."

"Vampires and aliens, Nattie? You were scared of them both?"

"Arlo, I'm trying to look real and you're distracting me—"

"Sorry, keep going."

"And she said, 'Natalie, it's so narcissistic. I mean why out of six billion people do you think aliens would choose you, anyway?'"

"I would."

Click of my stilettos on wet porcelain. The oily, botanic scent of the soap. I must have pressed a button on the phone and now the dial tone hummed against my cheek as I held it there, still. On the mosaic tile of the countertop was a pair of thin gold hair clips, abruptly familiar. The yellow tiles, interposed with occasional glitter-flecked white. Eggshells and yolk.

"Choose you," he said. "Out of six billion." He said that, but he didn't. Now his forehead was against mine, only for a moment. Closed my eyes, closed my hand over the hem of his shirt, the press of his lips to mine so quick it was hardly a kiss. A moist chill to his

NOT THE SAME ROAD OUT

skin, like after a fever breaks, and he stood back. "I think I should tell you something, Nattie. Things got kind of weird with Letizia last night."

This is just a thought, this is not real. Lana had offered these words as a sort of repetitious invocation and I recite them faithfully all through our morning hike down the Lookout Trail at Beamer Memorial. *This is just a thought* as we stop to marvel at wildflowers, blue flag iris and yellow pond lilies like scoops of butter, cool under the green trees. *This is not real.* Arlo refusing to climb up to an observation deck with a view of the Niagara Escarpment, too high up, and Finley says, "I can stay with him." Breathing the sap smell of spruce as Letizia and I go on alone. *This is not . . .* Signs along the way *do not move any rocks* and I think of the whole place tumbling like Jenga pieces. Letizia and I standing there for what feels like a long time looking out over the green spears of pine trees, the escarpment veiled in mist, unreal.

Back at the cottage, Finley says, "Thanks for showing us the area."

"It's a nice little trek," Arlo says. "Peaceful. Reminds me of the limestone caves in Lion's Head that Letizia and I visited last summer."

Finley nods. "But do you think they're technically caves? I feel like you would actually classify them as grottos."

"Whatever." Arlo opens the coffee canister. "I'm not a cave scientist."

"A speleologist," I say. Feeling the vague need to defend Finley, who seems unbothered, so why am I? As Letizia and I came down from the lookout, they were talking. Finley saying, "When I used to play hockey, it was different," and Arlo's low smirking voice, "But did you actually even play hockey, really? Weren't you just a goon? An easy bleed for boorish thrills. Did you ever even put the puck in the net?"

"There are different ways to even the score," Finley said. His gaze swept the white cedar trees above us. "Is that a Western Tanager? This place is great for birds."

Back in the kitchen, Arlo stops measuring the ground coffee. "You guys must be a lot of fun at Scrabble."

"Nattie," Letizia says, "maybe now is a good time for you and Arlo's session."

I point at the clock on the wall, a confusing wooden rectangle with scattered numbers of various sizes. "I have to call the girls," I say, although I've had no idea what time the clock is trying to signal since we've come here.

"After lunch, then," Letizia says, mixing coconut milk in her coffee. They are both dairy-free now, I remembered that from our text message conversations. Letizia's skin has never looked better, her tone perfect.

"Definitely," I say.

After lunch, Letizia pins me down. "Now," she says. "You and Arlo should do it now. Get it over with."

The therapy Arlo has recently been trained in promises to use rapid eye movements, meant to mimic the flickering of dream sleep, to reprogram the mind. To revise memories catalogued as traumatic, refile them in a happier place. When Letizia explained it all I'd thought of a mental junk drawer, cluttered with broken, sharp recollections.

I'd tried to stay on the phone with the girls as long as I could. "Amelia's hand got slammed under the blocks and I'm not sorry because she put her hand there on purpose," Daisy said, and I said, "It's not your fault but you should still feel for her that she got hurt." Sometimes I felt that so much of motherhood was just begging them to not grow up sociopathic, without a heart.

But eventually they'd run off and I'd run out of reasons to remain

NOT THE SAME ROAD OUT

in the loft. Now Arlo and I sit down in the living room. In the kitchen, Finley and Letizia talk about the best dairy substitute, which they both agree is coconut milk. Arlo, on the sofa, slides consent forms into a file.

"I don't think I really need to sign these forms," I say.

"It's part of the ethical conduct of my profession."

I want to say, "But you're not really a therapist yet," but I don't. Instead I take his leaky pen, scrawl my name along the line, a blotch of ink darkening my fingers, and feel, for a moment, the way I do in the backyard when my daughters offer cups full of dirt and tell me to pretend it's coffee.

"Are you ready?"

I nod, try not to rock in the unsteady chair, but it tilts. The idea of this therapy I like, an accelerated resolution.

"You have to really focus. Letizia mentioned you're dealing with anxiety, that you might want to address the birth—"

"She said we don't have to talk about it."

"You can just visualize —"

"Got it," I say, with no intention to think of Daisy either, afraid even if I leave things unspoken, Arlo might somehow be able to permeate my thoughts, like a ghost passing through walls. I just had to follow his hands with my eyes, Letizia had said. "Like hypnosis?" I'd asked, and she'd scoffed, "Of course not." I was disappointed. Instead it was something about how bilateral eye movements would somehow shuttle my bad thoughts away, replace them with what I'd wished had happened.

"There are limitations, of course," Arlo says. "You can't harm anyone, when you're visualizing."

"It would be unethical? Like it would go against your code?" I want to ask about confidentiality, if he would just run and tell Letizia everything if she wasn't already listening from the kitchen, but I don't. And Arlo nods, practising what I can tell is a look of integrity, all sincerity, the smirk gone from his lips, his sarcastic, almost nasty way of speaking now transmuted into something sage and altruistic.

"You can't kill anyone."

"I wouldn't."

"The focus needs to be on affirmative imagery."

"Looking on the bright side."

"If you want to reduce it to a basic platitude, then yes, Natalie." Arlo passes his hand back and forth, back and forth. Cooperatively, my eyes flick left to right. Maybe if I kept shoving things in my mental junk drawer it would eventually stop opening, like my real junk drawer in the kitchen. I keep my girls out of my thoughts. Instead I return to our cryptid class. Our professor had played the famous Patterson–Gimlin film, grainy footage of a female Bigfoot loping into the northern California forest before briefly glancing backwards. Left, right, left, the beautiful bipedal creature forever moving towards the treeline on a jittery loop.

The possibility of quick relief from this therapy had been suggested by the papers I'd signed, so when Arlo asks, "How do you feel now?" I nod in a way I hope appears serene. Letizia is watching, and I want to make her happy.

"Better, I think. Tranquil." Bob Gimlin and Roger Patterson, two rodeo riders, shot the footage in 1967. The less than sixty seconds of film and their subsequent notoriety sank their friendship.

"I appreciate your participation, Natalie," Arlo says.

"You can still call me Nattie."

"Nattie, your concentration was excellent."

"Yeah." Letizia's arms cross over her white lace top, her green and gold tile bracelets clacking. "Nattie's good at bullshitting."

They say the views here are to die for. The cottage high up on the Niagara Escarpment, far-reaching view of Georgian Bay. The sharp sweetness of pine. At dusk, deer move from the shadows, feeding on cedar branches.

I'm on the deck when Letizia comes out, barefoot in a cotton dress the bluish green of balsam fir, a slice of raw emerald on a gold chain. She doesn't say anything and I've never been that good with silence, so I say, "Strange place to visit with an acrophobic," something, anything, to occupy the quiet, so there are no empty spaces, like how they have those seat-fillers at the Oscars to fill the gaps.

"Arlo doesn't come back here." There isn't much grass beyond the deck before it drops off, a hundred feet of limestone cliffs. "That personal injury lawyer would love it here. Remember him?"

"Nicolo?"

"Yes. Is he still all over the billboards and bus stops in Windsor?"

"Everywhere."

"I love that. Remember that time we made Arlo take a picture of us in front of the billboard?"

"Yeah," I say. "Actually, I still have my copy."

"Really? I threw all those photos out years ago."

So still for a moment we can hear the quick whisk of bat wings in the trees over us. "I wasn't lying," I say, which we both know is another lie. "With Arlo. He seems good at what he does. What he's going to do, when he becomes a therapist."

"I shouldn't have said anything." Letizia perches in a deck chair, which is uncomfortable, built from twisted, shellacked twigs.

"Thanks for having us here."

"Okay." Letizia looks up at the sky, glitter on wet, dark paint. "Here's the truth. I was pretty messed up when I texted you about coming here. In the morning I was like shit, what did I do? At first, I didn't know how this would go."

I always took things too far. One brief conversation about a fresh coat of paint in Letizia's living room and I daydreamed we were the best friends on *Motel Makeover*, renovating rundown motels into boutique suites, drinking kombucha and thrifting the perfect gold vintage mirror.

"But I'm actually glad you came."

"Yeah," I say. "Me, too." A heavy feeling in my heart, bloated with sadness, like the sponge at the bottom of the kitchen sink with old dishwater, like a cloud on the cusp of rain.

If Letizia and Arlo and I had ever been any trinity at all it would have been Cerberus. Monstrous, venom in the mouth. Inside the cottage, Arlo is watching hockey with Finley. I climb the ladder to our loft. Vaulted ceiling and a skylight over the bed, a damp cedar smell. The quilt with its black bear and pine tree motif, the chalk-painted mason jars filled with dried daisies. Everything so perfect here.

The ladder creaks concerningly as it does under the weight of anyone who climbs it. Finley heaves himself up. "Are you going to bed already?"

"We shouldn't have come here."

Finley takes his things out. The different combs, the conditioner, the magnifying glass. "Sit up," he says, settling on the bed behind me.

"I don't have lice."

"Nat, you know regular inspection is part of preventative care."

When he'd been training for his new job, a decade ago now, we practised every night. Finley doesn't believe in the chemicals, the medicated cream rinses. Instead, when he removes the lice, he does it all by hand, wet combing, detaching each egg, so tiny you could fit two on a pinhead. The first comb detangles. He parts my hair with his fingers, clips it into quadrants.

Bob and Roger reconciled in the end, but only while Roger lay dying. Roger begging Bob to promise him they'd go back to California. By the next day he was dead. Their names are still always tangled together. You think of one when you think about the other. I wonder if Bob dreamed, after, of the creek bed in California, horseback again. *Wait*, I always wanted to say when Letizia's messages would stop, *Where are you going? There is still so much I want to say to you.* But I was understanding it might never be here again. That it could maybe only be in dream sleep, where our hearts accelerate, and our closed eyes see.

Finley picks up the thin steel lice comb and works quietly, strand by strand. Each long stroke of the comb is lulling, reassuring, teeth to the root and then again. Scent of lavender, geranium, tea tree oil, misting my damp hair.

"All clear," he says, and I want to believe him.

Invasive Species

LILLIAN AU

Northwest Territories | Canol Heritage Trail,
City of Yellowknife–Frame Lake Trail

A helicopter touches down in a remote gravel valley at the base of the Mackenzie Mountains, about 250 kilometres southwest of Norman Wells, in early September, the end of the Dall sheep hunting season. Two men carrying backpacks and a dog hop out and make their way deep into the unspoiled wilderness. They want to press forward, but they are forced to stop and find a place to camp. They have a mandatory twelve-hour wait after being dropped off from the chopper before beginning their hunt. As soon as the morning sun lifts and grazes the land, they push off for higher elevation. The climb meanders at a slow, measured pace into the remote rocky landscape. They stop at a ridge where there's a 360-degree view. With their eyes trained behind the lens of their high-powered spotting scopes, they search for the elusive Dall sheep.

At the front is Björn Nygaard, a hunting guide, followed by his client, Johannes Berger. Johannes is a veterinarian from Yellowknife who specializes in injury-prone racing dogs from top sled teams and overweight household pets. Björn's dog, Bullet, takes up the rear as he zigzags in and out of the water of a creek bed.

Björn turns around to make sure Johannes is keeping up with him. It's not the first time he's taken a veterinarian out to stalk sheep, caribou, moose, and wolf. Johannes is different. As a resident

NOT THE SAME ROAD OUT

of the Northwest Territories, he could legally hunt on his own. However, it would be nearly impossible for him to find a target, and he knows it. It is easier and faster to have an expert sheep hunter who knows the area at his side.

Most of Björn's clients—ninety percent of whom are from the United States—would be lost if they were dumped in the middle of nowhere. They're also not used to hiking and climbing ten to fifteen miles a day in sheep country. Dall sheep like to hang out in deep grassy slopes, close to rocks in steep, protected areas away from wolves and grizzly bears. Warmed by the midnight sun, the black shale rocks are a favourite spot for the sheep to paw out and bed down.

Johannes, who grew up reading every book written by Jack O'Connor, always dreamed of hunting big game. He has kept up the strict fitness regime from his days as a competitive ski jumper in Austria and has no problem matching Björn's quick pace.

Björn starts to pull back as he feels a familiar tightness in his chest. He ignores it. It passes, and he pushes forward, sure-footed.

On a plateau next to a cluster of jagged rocks plush with lichen, Björn finds a perch with an unobstructed view of the valley. He blinks furiously every couple of minutes to give his eyes a break from looking through the lens of his high-powered binoculars. Both men spend several hours searching in a grid pattern for a twitching ear or any other sign of movement hidden in the dark shale. But the rams remain out of sight.

They drop off into a new valley, climb up, and run ridges for places to spot. At a rocky bluff with good sightlines, they throw their packs down. The leftovers of a meal—chewed up feathers and bone fragments—form a debris field on the ground. Whatever left the remains behind didn't linger. Bullet sniffs at the feathers and expresses his disinterest by sitting beside Björn's backpack.

"Reckon a fox or wolf got to it? What do you think? Funny

looking bird. No way would I eat it. Ptarmigan maybe," Johannes says.

Björn shrugs. "That looks to be a short-tailed shearwater. Should be on its way migrating down south, like to Tasmania, and not up here. There were sightings of them in Inuvik and Nunavut. Yeah, it's strange . . ." Björn pauses. He doesn't want raise any alarm but he figures Johannes is a vet and it would be better if he knew what was out there.

"Wild pig got it. Hard to believe. Look at the tracks on the dirt. Hooves are the size of a teacup. These birds don't belong here. Same with the pigs."

Johannes surveys the leftover meal again. This time in disgust. "Pffft. These wild pigs are a menace—four-legged rototillers, spreading disease and destroying crops. A few of them have had a run-in with some of the sled dogs I look after. I didn't know they were this far up north." He shakes his head.

It's not the first time wild pigs and southern birds have been spotted outside Norman Wells and elsewhere in the Northwest Territories. With temperatures five degrees above normal for August, what was strange is becoming familiar. Björn won't hunt the same area in a season to ensure the number of local rams aren't depleted. But seeing signs of animals that belong down south in the mountains is odd but, as long as they kept their distance, it isn't his problem. What have always been problems are grizzly bears and cubs. Björn's body clenches. His face hardens as he clamps down on a lurching memory. His good hand searches for Bullet, a compact blue heeler with a one-eyed mask, who nudges him back.

Björn didn't come by his name by accident. His Swedish parents named him Bear to convey strength, courage, and power. It helped that he looked like a cuddly brown bear when he was a baby. Even now, Björn's lollipop head, shaggy burnt-caramel-coloured hair and feral brown eyes gave him a wild appearance. Looks aside, it's his

NOT THE SAME ROAD OUT

skill tracking sheep and his ninety-five percent find-rate that attracts people like Johannes, who pay $50,000 for a ten-day guided hunt. As one of only two vets in Yellowknife, Johannes can afford it. This is his first time out with Björn—he's been on a wait list for years. Johannes believes no apology is necessary for killing big game. On average, sheep live ten to twelve years, max. The hunters go after only mature rams, knowing if they didn't kill them, mother nature would finish the job. It is finally his turn and he is more than ready. Dressed in camo gear, Johannes carefully wipes his Swarovski spotting scope. "Let me clean your binos," he offers.

Björn slowly bends forward and lets the vet remove the strap from his neck without a word. With only one good hand, it takes Björn a little longer to do things. He's not the same person he was two summers ago. The bear attack keeps looping in his head, over and over: the casual walk to the base camp outhouse, the beast's wet, fetid breath, the searing pain as the bear's teeth clamped on his right hand. While Björn lay helpless on the ground, Bullet attacked and chased the animal away.

Only his right thumb was spared. Good enough to hitch a ride into town but too gimped up to hold a gun steady. He no longer carries his lever action 30-30 rifle, relying on the dog instead. Bullet had attached himself to Björn, a self-appointed bodyguard rewarded with plenty of dog treats. He wasn't a pet to mess around with.

It's the fourth day of their hunt, with over fifty kilometres of ground covered. They've spotted twenty-nine sheep but they were either too young or long gone by the time they maneuvered into shooting range. Undeterred, they climb another valley finding a perch halfway up a mountainside.

Björn lets the quiet settle and they wait. After a few hours, he spots a band of sheep bedded down over the top, about four kilometres away. The two men take their time and move in slowly.

INVASIVE SPECIES

Another two hours pass. They are about four hundred metres away when Johannes accidentally kicks a pile of loose rocks. He freezes, but it doesn't matter. The sheep are used to hearing rocks breaking away.

The wind blows stiff in their face, away from their cover. The largest ram looks to be about ten years old with double flaring, full-curl horns.

"He's good-looking. Decent size. What do you think?" Johannes asks nervously.

"He's big, got a pot belly and sway back. I count ten rings on the horn. Yup. This is the one." Björn motions to Johannes to get ready. "Stay on the animal. Take your time. Deep breath," he coaches softly.

Johannes's hands shake as he grips the rifle. His breathing is ragged. It's his first time pointing a rifle at a Dall sheep.

"I wish I took up biathlon instead of ski-jumping growing up," he jokes.

"You're doing good. You have him in sight."

There are two ewes sleeping and three rams standing and chewing their cud. The older ram stops between two evergreens, alert and looking straight at the hunters.

"Steady? We have time. If it's not right. Let's fix it up," Björn cautions.

Johannes nods impatiently. "It's good."

"Take the second one from the right. Do you see him?"

"Yes, I'm on him," Johannes replies. His hands are sweaty. It's hard for him to contain his excitement. Björn whispers, "Do it."

As soon as the words leave his mouth, Björn wants to take them back. He snaps his eyes shut against an unexpected jolt of despair. He's watched so many ancient animals buckle, trying to hold on before free-falling to the ground. He doesn't want to witness another one.

NOT THE SAME ROAD OUT

The Kimber cracks the air, but a sudden movement from below causes the ram to swerve and bolt. The bullet lands a few degrees left of the intended target. Too far off to drop the animal.

A hairy streak of black springs out from nowhere. The rest of the sheep scatter. "*Verdammt! Scheiße*," Johannes swears.

Björn flips his eyes open. A wild pig scampers back and forth, strutting an invisible runway, its skinny spitz tail twirling like a middle finger. The pig is built like a mini-flatbed truck. Its stocky body is covered with a coarse rug of spiky black hair, and a pair of tusks shaped like Ginsu knives stick out on either side of its flaring snout. Björn swears hit is grinning. Bullet takes off in pursuit.

Johannes takes aim in disgust and fires off a row of angry, jerky shots, then tosses his gun down. "Where did it come from?" He wipes a sheen of sweat from under his nose.

Björn doesn't answer at first. He's rattled by pig sighting and the dead bird—anomalies in these parts—and by a mutinous sense of relief. The old ram gets to live another day. "Bad luck," he says. "Not your fault. Your aim was spotless. You're no Dick Cheney. That pig came from nowhere and spooked them."

Bullet circles back to Bjorn's side, his tongue hanging out in defeat, just like Johannes.

The vet looks gutted. "That old ram was mine. *Mine!* Now gone. Pouf! All that time wasted thanks to that ugly piece of schnitzel." He shakes his head with frustration. "Hard to believe these pigs are this far north. *Das ist verrückt.*"

Björn's secret satisfaction turns to uneasiness. "It's too cold for them in the winter here. Should be gone soon, back to Alberta or Saskatchewan. Just a slight setback. Best to retreat and come back tomorrow."

It takes Johannes another two days to bag his trophy. With the sun beating down on them, the men wait it out, taking turns scanning the mountainside. Blurry waves of late-season heat lift, and a band of eight rams are spotted in the shade of a scree, where they've bedded down on some fine black shale to keep cool. No swine sightings this time. The men weave in and around the rocks before climbing into position above the rams. From a distance of two hundred metres, Johannes nails an eleven-year-old ram between the shoulders with a dull wallop. It cartwheels like a gymnast, end over end, slamming into the cliffs and shale on its way down the mountain. The moment seems to last forever, until the pirouette of the ram's flailing legs crumples into the rocks with a thud.

"Hell yeah! Got 'im. Let's go."

Bjorn puts his hand up.

"Stay put, Berger. We gotta make sure it's dead." He shoots him a hard look. "Put your safety on."

"*Ja, ja.* But it's not moving."

"We still have to wait. Look, some of the other rams are hanging around."

"Why? What does it matter?"

"That dead ram was probably the leader. They don't know what to do. They need to sort themselves out and find another leader."

It doesn't take long before two rams start to butt heads for the top job. Others stretch or take a pee before bedding down. With the old leader out of sight, the rams chew their cud like nothing happened.

"I hope the horns didn't break. That was quite a distance he fell."

"Don't worry. I have electrical tape. If that doesn't do the job, the taxidermist can glue it back. They're pros."

"Speaking of pro, it was a perfect one-shot kill, wasn't it? That was phenomenal. Ha. ha!" Johannes gloats.

Björn doesn't respond.

After ten minutes, Björn nods his head. Johannes takes off with the same explosive push he used to on skis. He scrambles over the rocks, eager to claim his prize. The ram's tongue has flopped out; his

NOT THE SAME ROAD OUT

eyes are open but lifeless. It was a big fella. Even bigger and better up close.

"*Eins, zwei, drei...*"

Johannes exhales when he counts to *elf*. There are eleven growth rings on the thankfully unbroken, prehistoric-looking horns. He can't help petting the ram and running his fingers through its matted fur. A streak of bright red points to where the bullet punched the pillowy softness of the sheep's belly, a rose on a carpet of white fur.

Johannes takes out two one-ounce bottles of Jägermeister and offers one to Björn. The Austrian chugs his down in one gulp, wipes his mouth with the back of his hand, and releases a full-throated bellow of laughter that echoes down the valley.

The buzz of the kill is fleeting. The remorse lingers. Björn examines the dead ram with forced detachment. He will have to butcher it quickly before it gets too dark. He lets his client savour this moment while he checks on his skinning knives. He wants to get on with it, head back.

Johannes starts to speak, but his voice catches. He clears his throat awkwardly, clasps his hands together and inhales deeply. "Thank you for the life you have given us. This magnificent creature lived long, and we are blessed to be in its presence. I am grateful to be on this journey and at the end of this circle of life. Thank you for giving me the strength to scale this mountain, to bear witness to this remarkable creature, and receive the gift of this land. I am humbled and honoured." Then he lets out a holler and whistles.

Dead eyes gleam as the vet props the massive, drooping head up for selfies. The dead ram is frowning, its broken teeth flashing against its milky alpine pelage.

"I have some dental floss." Johannes offers.

"No, I'm good." Björn takes a needle and thread from his sewing kit, pokes a hole in the ram's upper and lower gums, threads it, and ties a loop to clamp the ram's mouth closed. It's the only kind of sewing he does. He could have wrapped dental floss around the snout instead, but the muscle of the ram's mouth wouldn't sit as naturally. Björn wants the ram to look perfect. He takes photos from every angle, a celebratory ritual, then steps back and watches his client soak in the glory. Berger's on the satellite phone talking to base camp to break the good news.

"Textbook stalk. You nailed it." Björn follows the script, flattering the client's ego. He should shake Berger's hand but pulls back at the last minute. He puts on a smile and jerks his thumb up from his fingerless mitt.

It always feels anticlimactic when a hunt is over but it's never bothered Björn before. He has spent all his life hunting and guiding. His father always made sure the freezer was full of venison, caribou, and elk from the land. Björn has never gone to bed with an empty stomach or stepped out in the bitter cold without the layered warmth of fur skinned by his father's hands or his own. The animal didn't suffer and it was a clean kill.

Still, all he feels now is shame, adrenalin replaced by a dull ache. His heart patters wildly. His breathing is ragged. A wave of fatigue washes over him. Maybe he'll finally get around to seeing a doctor when he flies back into Yellowknife. Marie keeps begging him to get checked out. He takes a gulp of water and sits on a rock to make sure he doesn't fall. Quiet, crouching thoughts stalk him as he slowly turns toward the spot above where the ram toppled over. There's nothing, then something. He squints. An apparition of the old ram stares at him accusingly. Is he losing his mind?

Berger is still on the phone reliving his victory. The raucous laughter pulls him back to the task at hand. He's not used to feeling guilty and tries to shake it off by getting up and pulling on a pair of disposable gloves. He takes his skinning knife and gets to work like he's on the line in a meat processing plant. It will take him an hour to package what's left of the ram into meat bags. He sets aside

NOT THE SAME ROAD OUT

a few pieces of the tenderloin. The rib cage with the spine running through it and the innards are left behind.

The men collect some wood from a stand of trees near the base of the cliff and cook the tenderloin over a campfire. Stomachs full, they spend their final evening at the kill site until a helicopter picks them up and flies them to base camp. The next day, they take off for Norman Wells to check in with the Fish and Game Warden. With a paper tag notched and a plug drilled to the back of the ram's horn, Berger is cleared to fly back to Yellowknife, his dead-eyed souvenir sticking out from the top of his backpack. He shakes Björn's hand, pats Bullet on the head, and passes a fat tip to the guide. On top of his generous pay from the guide outfitting company, Björn will be able to live off the money all winter without working.

Björn spends the last couple of weeks of the season closing down the base camp outside Norman Wells. He winterizes the cook shack and shower house, and disconnects the solar panels. Bundles of firewood are collected, and all the hunting gear is cleaned and put away.

It's late October when he and Bullet fly home back to Yellowknife. At the arrivals lounge, a giant stuffed polar bear stands guard on top of a baggage carousel. Björn averts his eyes and searches for his hockey bag, which comes spitting out and sliding down the chute in no time. Outside the airport, Björn spots Marie waiting in her pickup truck. It's parked right next to another truck with the logo of a construction company contracted to clean up Giant Mine. A child has written "clean me" in big letters on the dusty window. He is adding a happy face when his mother arrives.

"Ezra, don't touch that truck! It's contaminated with arsenic. What did I tell you? You have to be careful!" She yanks sheets of wet wipes from a container in her purse and scrubs the kid's fingers over and over.

Björn gets in the truck and gives Marie a peck on the cheek. "A bit overprotective, don't ya think? Feel sorry for that kid. He can't wipe his ass without his mom's permission."

Björn met Marie at the hospital after the bear attack. "I hear ya sure pissed off some bear, eh? He sure scrambled your hand. Better not piss me off. I'm from the Bear clan. Roll over, please." Björn lifted his injured hand and flopped over like a seal, the painkillers making him clumsy. She looked beautiful despite the dark bags under her eyes and her stained uniform. There's nothing like having someone give you a shot in the butt to overcome shyness.

After surgery and two days of recuperation, Björn worked up the nerve to ask Marie out on his last day. "I'm not going to miss the food here, but I'll miss talking to you. Maybe, when you're off work, you might be free to ah um . . . go for coffee?"

Coffee morphed into more dates, moving in, and with Marie's care, Björn had returned to work. That was two years ago.

"Hey, buddy! I miss you." Marie gives Bullet a scratch behind the ear when he jumps in the truck. He does a couple of revolutions on the spot before he settles in the seat behind Björn. Marie doesn't waste time.

"You look tired. Pale even. What's going on with your chest?"

"Just some aches and pains."

"Sure." Marie's voice drips with doubt. "Just to be on the safe side, I booked an appointment for you at the clinic. You're not backing out this time."

Björn rolls his eyes and rubs Bullet's back. The dog is straining out the window, half his body in the air. Before starting the engine, Marie says, "I wouldn't let Bullet lick that truck if you ask me."

Marie has a trapline in Dettah, not far from the contaminated mine site. She used to forage for berries and mushrooms there, but stopped despite reassurances from the government officials that the arsenic concentrations in the air are safe. Marie still remembers a news story about a boy who died from eating snow near the mine in the 1950s. Björn spent last winter helping Marie check the traps for the muskrat, martens, weasel, and wolves that still come through. They sold the pelts but didn't eat the meat.

The truck rumbles over the potholes past City Hall and Frame Lake where toxic sediment swirls below the thin crème brûlée surface of water beginning to freeze. No longer host to fish and swimmers, the lake is dead, killed by arsenic trioxide and sulfur dioxide that used to spew out of the tall smokestacks and seep into the water like tea leaves in a pot. Where the mine once stood, underground chambers containing tons of toxic waste remain, buried there for almost three-quarters of a century. The First Nations people call the poisonous dust *Nagha,* sleeping monster.

November winds down and temperatures dip to -25°, good enough to travel over the frozen lakes. Despite Marie's protests, Björn jumps on his skidoo and spends the next few days setting traps and repairing the one burned a wildfire during the summer. When he returns a week later, the traps are half empty, surrounded by shards of bone and scraps of fur.

"Pigs," he says, shaking his head in disgust.

Björn would never have guessed he would hear the word "pig" coming out of his doctor's mouth a week later.

"You have a leaky aortic valve and need surgery immediately. Since you're allergic to the coating on titanium, your only choice is to have a living valve inserted from a pig."

The cardiologist's mouth flaps like a fish sucking in oxygen. Björn stops listening after he hears the word pig. He thinks of the smart-alecky pig that saved the old ram on the last hunt of the season. Maybe it was trying to tell him something. *Pigs are lifesavers.* Hard to believe, but then the doctor starts rattling on about how common this type of operation is and it is normal to use pig, sheep, and cow implants. It's not a hard sell; Björn wants to live. He's grateful his bacon is going to be saved by a pig of all things.

Björn is sent down to Edmonton where his chest is sawed open like a chicken breastbone. Under the bright operating lights, his eraser-pink heart beats feebly as a valve from a freshly killed pig is sewn in. Under sedation, Björn has an out-of-body experience and is visited again by the dead ram.

"Save the p—," bleats a deep gravelly voice. His chest looks like a red wine stain spilled on white carpet. Björn is unable to make out the last word. He thinks the ram was trying to say, "Save the pigs."

After a few days recuperating in the hospital, Björn is well enough to fly back to Yellowknife. He tries to shut out the bleating words he heard on the operating table, but he can't forget, especially when he looks down at his chest. The angry red scar and stitches are a reminder of the pig valve underneath his skin keeping him alive. No longer needing a wheelchair, he takes his first steps outside. His heart beats solidly like the quick, snappy beat of the short-tailed shearwaters darkening the sky. *What are they still doing here?* It's the middle of winter. They should be in Australia, not the subarctic.

The sky is pleated with rows of undulating clouds. He was told there's a name for it: a mackerel sky. Above normal temperatures and rain is forecast. He remembers the fish scales of the white fish he and his father would catch off Yellowknife Bay. That was before they were told the fish were no longer safe to eat.

The tight-clenched grip of winter surrenders to the creep of spring. It's early March, and Marie is back on the trapline. She works alone. Björn tells her he's quit hunting and trapping.

"Are you off your meds?" Marie shakes her head in disbelief. Ever since Björn had his surgery, he's been acting weird. Even Bullet can sense something is off—not just with Björn but the land. The trees lean drunkenly on top of ragged seams of decaying Canadian shield rock. Marie is forced to park the skidoo and walk into the trapline because there's not enough snow. The snares are empty again. Patches of threadbare snow knit the land and hide the slumping frozen ground underneath. Marie shakes her head in disappointment and surprise. Where are all the animals? Did the pigs get to them again?

As the days grow longer, the thawing permafrost surrenders to the sun's baking heat. Collapsed earth morphs into rivers of broken mud and rock. The heat awakens a new kind of enemy from below the ground and above.

At first, a wild pig spotted in Yellowknife fails to raise any alarm bells. It could almost pass for a fat dog from a distance. Soon there are sightings of wild pigs running past houseboats, the float planes and over the causeway into Latham Island. Wallowing in the thawing snow, the porkers have a merry old time barging through town at the fast-food drive thru, circling the RCMP station, and hanging out at the dump.

Björn, with his new pig's heart valve, thinks they can do no wrong even when they're destroying crops and nets and spreading diseases. Marie can't stand the new Björn and gives him an ultimatum: shoot the pigs on their trapline or leave. Björn moves into a trailer park, hoping Marie will grow to tolerate the pigs.

With Björn's help, a few of the pigs sport leftover dog booties and coats thrown out by a dog kennel. They become emboldened, claiming the right of way on the sidewalk, forcing residents to sidestep.

The ravens won't leave the pigs alone. Both creatures are territorial and feud over the garbage. Piercing screeches and the thrashing of powerful wings beating overhead compete with angry grunts and squeals from the ground. The birds dive and careen like water bombers while the pigs zigzag from their hiding places. Seeing the mêlée, Björn runs out with his broom and tries to swat the birds away from his precious pigs.

INVASIVE SPECIES

The city's residents are divided: should the pigs be shot or left alone? Most of the members of the Islamic Centre of Yellowknife are on Team Raven. They argue that the birds were here first and insist the pigs be corralled and shipped out of town. Others call for a pig cull. Animal rights activists fly in from Vancouver to defend the rights of the wild pigs, arguing they were God's creatures, and pigs and people could learn to co-exist.

While residents choose a side, and politicians argue over the wording of a motion about the fate of the swine, the pigs multiply until they outnumber the people. Out of an abundance of caution, pig days are called at schools and children are forced to stay home. A $2,000 bounty per pig snout is announced. But the pigs evade capture and continue to squat on the land in circles, like Druids.

Back on the trapline, Marie notices dead pigs floating on the surface of the lakes and another one half-buried in the melting snow. There is no sign of a gunshot wound.

She calls Björn. "Get over here. You have to see this. Something has happened to the pigs."

They bring the carcass to Berger's clinic. The sheep horns hang at the entrance, above the reception desk.

"Arsenic. This pig was poisoned," the vet declares. "Probably the rest of them you saw too, Marie. I have to report this to the Department of Health and Wildlife. This is troubling." Berger shakes his head with worry.

"Do you think it's from the mine?" Marie asks.

"Dunno. Have to test the groundwater. I suspect it's leaching from the mine site. If the permafrost is breaking down, we have a catastrophe on our hands."

Björn interrupts. "It's coming from the storage containers? I thought the supplementary cooling system was keeping them frozen?"

"System failure. It relies on recycled cold air. A 1.5° rise in temperature or higher starts a chain reaction. All that arsenic buried underground will start to thaw."

As the weight of his words sink in, Björn feels his heart race. His new pig valve flutters. He looks at Marie. His eyes gleam with regret.

"That's what the ram was telling me. The pigs didn't need saving. It was right before me. The wounded land, like the ram, bleeding and dying in front of me."

"Did you say you were talking to a ram?" Marie looks at him strangely.

"These pigs are opportunists and are simply feeding on what we've left. It's our fault."

June 21: the longest day of the year. The glare of the sun follows—it's everywhere. Residents used to celebrate the summer solstice with a festival that lasted well into the night. Now they're busy packing. When the houses on concrete pilings start to collapse and the roads buckle and sink into the mushy ground, panic sets in. Berger grabs his sheep trophy before closing up his business.

A few years ago, it was a summer of smoke and flames that forced the population of Yellowknife to flee. This year it's a pig invasion and the Big Melt. Under the midnight sun, *Nagha* awakens.

Marie has to persuade Björn to get into the pickup truck. He doesn't want to go, but eventually they join the exodus of vehicles crawling along on Highway 3. The line-up stretches for miles, creeping along, leaving the scarred, poisoned landscape behind.

They pass a lone caribou sauntering along the side of the highway. In the rearview mirror, a pig wallows in mud before getting up and lifting one leg to mark the "Welcome to Yellowknife" sign.

Bullet howls.

Red Shoes in the Dust

TERRY WATADA

Alberta | Meadowlark Rail Trail

The view from the front door was heartbreaking. Before him was a wide expanse of barren fields, with clumps of dirt barely holding up dry, shrivelled, and stunted tufts of alien plants. It reached to the curvature of the earth. The sky above was a bright, clear blue, so intense it hurt the eyes. Even if they were "zip eyes," he still had to shade them with his hands. That morning was the first the ten-year-old saw his surroundings in the clear light of day. So different from Sandon and Vancouver it made his head dizzy. He took a couple of steps down the rickety stairs and heard a long, sad wind whistling, whining across the land. It kicked up a lot of ghostly dust. He felt the wind on his face and breathed in the faint, imagined scent of a distant dark forest, flowing water, and majestic mountains. He was strangely homesick for their shack some great distance away, to him anyway, in British Columbia. He missed Hiro most of all.

Hideki and his parents had arrived the night before in a broken-down fisherman's truck owned by a family friend who was also making his way to this desert called Alberta. The pungent smell of dead fish stayed with him a long time. How old man Takahashi found his way through the darkness was beyond him. Hideki found comfort in knowing his father would be awake all night, sitting next to Takahashi-*san*, making sure they were safe. At some point, Hideki, cradled in his mother's arms, had fallen asleep and dreamed of the forests of Sandon, his home for the past four years. And of the streets of Vancouver, the home where he'd been born.

Did Takahashi-*san* dream of the sea, Hideki wondered in a dream. The old fisherman from Steveston had a dead wife, was a cousin of Hideki's mother, and had no children. Like the Watanabes, Takahashi-*san* was leaving Sandon now that the war was over and there was nothing for him there or in the province. He'd volunteered to drive Hideki's family in his banged-up truck.

Hideki's family was starting life anew as sharecroppers in this place some distance from Irricana, Alberta, a small hamlet of a few hundred people. North of the town was the farm, with a barn and a house nearby. It was owned by the Stacks, who had no kids. They were standoffish and acted as if it was a favour they were doing, never mind that the government was paying them rent. Mr. Stack had a dour face; his wife was rotund and never smiled. The Watanabes were generally left alone, except Dad, who worked for Mr. Stack in the fields.

They lived in a chicken shack, cheap wood and chicken wire around. Cracks and holes everywhere, worse than Sandon, if that were possible. He imagined the cold wind of winter entering with icy fingers. His father worked to plug the holes. The floor and walls were splattered with the animal leavings. There had been days of cleaning to be done. The smell had been so intense, Hideki's mom never ate chicken again. There was a potbelly stove to keep things toasty—early spring on the prairies was cold. There was a rustic wooden table and chairs for dining. Their beds (three) were simple frames with wooden slats to support the provided mattresses. They were old and smelled it. Hideki's mom had thought to bring sheets and pillows so there was a reminder of home. The "kitchen" was rough, a counter with some cooking utensils. Mom also had wisely brought her own implements. There was a wood stove besides the potbelly one for cooking. Water had to be brought in from a nearby well. Hideki's chores: bring in firewood and fresh water daily.

There was a train station in town, but no train ever came by. The building itself had seen better days—the only platform was worn with cracks in the planks, the green-tiled roof needed replacement, and the interior was full of dust and tumbleweeds, the office furniture and chairs mostly gone. What remained was smashed into bits. Rumour had it that the station was soon to be closed permanently. "But we're here!" Hideki complained to his father. When he watched the occasional, seemingly lost train pass through, the isolation froze his core even more.

Hideki suspected the white folk there did not like to see the likes of him. Probably kill him on sight. He was the enemy, even after Hiroshima and Nagasaki had exploded with impossible fury, destroying everything. He was still a dirty Jap, imprisoned and forgotten for the sake of Canada's safety. There was not much hope for him in Irricana, and no warmth in the early spring light. Life here was worse than Sandon, Hideki concluded.

A deep sense of alienation set into the core of the young boy, especially when he walked the lonely tracks that led into town. Near the Stack's farm, they sank into the landscape until a vanishing point. In Irricana, where his new school stood, he saw men, some women and even fewer children, none of whom looked like him. His stomach tingled with fear.

He yearned to see someone his age who was his kind, Japanese Canadian. He found it odd that he missed the internment camp in BC.

Sandon was located between two tributary ranges of the Selkirk Mountains in southeastern British Columbia. The ghost town, with its collection of barely standing shacks and a ramshackle three-storey city hall perched on a small hill overlooking a roaring Carpenter

Creek, was used as an internment camp for Japanese Canadians. The settlement was wedged between the mountains near the top of the valley. Sunlight was scarce (between four to six hours a day), everyone found, because of the towering rock walls on either side. And the constant wind was ice cold. Local miners called it the "Devil's breath."

The government, in its wisdom, at first decided to segregate the Japanese by religion. Sandon was for the Buddhists, Lemon Creek for the Catholics, New Denver the Protestants. Some of the community leaders had wondered if there would be enough space, since most of the Japanese Canadians were Buddhists. The camp initially held about one thousand internees.

Hideki and his parents lived in one of the dilapidated miner's shacks hauled from some unknown location. Though grateful for a place to stay, they had to spend the first several weeks cleaning it. Before his father had joined him and his mother in the camp, male friends had applied their carpentry skills to build furniture. Other volunteers plugged the holes in the roof and walls. After four years, it was livable, if more than a little primitive.

For the first two years in Sandon, Hideki and his mother were alone. Dad had been arrested and kidnapped by the Mounties from their apartment in Vancouver in the middle of the night in the spring of '42. They were never told where they had taken him or the charges against him. His mom said it was for the way he "looked." There hadn't been a day that went by that Hideki didn't hide to worry and cry about his father. In the meantime, mom and son travelled to Sandon without him.

When the family finally reunited near the end of the second year, Hideki asked his dad where he had been, but *Otousan* didn't want to talk. He turned to his mother, but she was equally silent. She probably didn't know.

Others in the Sandon camp told him they were "Enemy Aliens," restricted to the area. He heard people could simply walk away, if they wanted to—there were no guards, no obvious military presence (just one older Mountie), no barbed wire, but where were they to go? Nothing but wild forest and rock for miles around. The New Denver internment camp was about ten miles away, close by. No use going there. Calgary in Alberta was the nearest city, but too far to travel to. Impractical. Besides, they would probably be arrested for not belonging there. Hideki remembered the white men with rifles who accompanied them as they made their way to Sandon. Grim and menacing, they were not welcoming at all. Probably the same wherever they went.

This was war. At eight years old, Hideki vaguely understood that since he looked like the enemy, he must be the enemy. By the time he was ten, he was confused. He was Japanese Canadian, born and raised in Vancouver. Wasn't he the *Canadian* part more than the *Japanese*?

Sandon was a remote prison, but the surrounding forests were clean-smelling, refreshing, and there was a rushing stream through the middle of the settlement. Darkness did come early, but no one said anything.

His fellow internees were many and mostly from Vancouver. Reverend Tsuji was the Buddhist priest there, the first Canadian-born, but he wasn't around much since he had to take care of the needs of Buddhists and even Christians around the province.

Loud and old, Mrs. Miyamoto with a history of losing husbands was in camp. Her caterwauling could be heard everywhere. Besides her voice, she was known for her catering skills and made delicious dishes for meetings (even with the meagre ingredients the government provided). Her three husbands had died accidentally over the years. No one talked about them. Hideki chuckled to himself when he thought they had been startled by her loud, booming voice and fell to their end. And there were the Shimizus, owners of Tak's

NOT THE SAME ROAD OUT

Confectionary Store on Powell Street in Vancouver's Japan Town. The missus gave him free candy every so often. Old Man Shimizu always frowned at him whether she did or not. They had a son, two years older than Hideki, Hiro. They were together at Strathcona school. The day both families were exiled from Vancouver to the other side of the province was the saddest day, at that point, in Hideki's life.

"Buck up, Hideki, old boy." Hiro was always cheery and confident. "You read the government poster – it's a temporary measure, for our protection."

"You believe that?" Hideki's face was scrunched with sorrow and worry.

"It's all we got."

"Yeah. But I don't know where we're all going. I might never see you again."

"Yeah. Don't worry, we'll find each other, eventually." Hiro was tall, taller than Hideki, and had a handsome face. All the girls thought so.

At least they were all together in Sandon.

As the end of the war approached and the government decided that segregation by religion posed a danger (a common belief might inspire protest and rebellion), the camps began to close. All Japanese Canadians were ordered to resettle. Though some went to New Denver, the majority moved east in exile, not back to their homes on the west coast. That was forbidden. All their property had been confiscated and sold to returning veterans for pennies on the dollar. He watched his father swear, beating the shack walls with his fists, while his mother cried.

A very few defied the order and stayed in Sandon, fending for themselves; Hideki's parents decided to move to Alberta. His dad found a poster advertising a job for farm hands. They were to be provided with a house and a decent wage. "No use staying here," he said. "We're being kicked out. No job prospects here . . ." That's when Takahashi-*san* offered a ride.

This farewell was worse than the first in Vancouver. This time, Hideki did not know where Hiro and his family were headed. He wouldn't even be able to write his friend letters. All he knew was that most, including Hiro, were headed into the vast eastern emptiness of Canada.

"We'll find each other again," a confident Hiro assured him. "Don't worry."

Hideki's round face was sad, poised to cry.

"We found each other in Sandon, right?"

All Hideki could do was nod his head in sadness. He hiccupped tears.

The two bowed to each other, clasped hands to shake a farewell.

He yearned for life in Vancouver before it had all started. The sights and smells of Powell Street on a Saturday. All the tussle and bustle filled his senses with the aroma of fresh-baked *pan*, kneaded *mochi* and cooked fish. The voices of friends and strangers infused the air with friendship and reverie.

Haramatsu-san? *How's your ingrown toenail? I hope you're getting better.*

Are you coming to the otera *tomorrow? The minister mentioned you by name. Big meeting after service.*

Good saba *at Union Fish. Just caught yesterday.*

Even Japanese language school lessons, every day after English school and on Saturday mornings, were filled with friends and horseplay at weekend recess—even if the serious Kozai *Sensei* kept a watchful eye with a handy long pointer and barked loud curses at miscreants.

What he missed most was Powell Ground, where the mighty Asahi baseball team played. He couldn't afford the fifteen cents to

NOT THE SAME ROAD OUT

sit in the stands, so he stood or rather sat on the grass just beyond third base.

Boy, that Roy Yamamura sure could hit a ball. A mile, I bet!

Hiro and Hideki played baseball, emulating their heroes. Hiro was the athlete. He could pitch fastballs like no other—Hideki's hand hurt when he caught one. Hiro could run the bases faster than anyone in school. He could swing a bat like Roy Yamamura. Hideki could see it in the way his friend stood at the plate waiting for the first pitch. He lowered his head at the memory, squeezing his eyes shut. Everything was disappearing, it seemed. A few tears seeped out and ran down his cheeks.

Even when Hideki ventured away from Powell Street, away from the safety of Japanese signs, language, Hiro, and his parents, and into the confines of downtown Vancouver, he was mesmerized by the array of stores and businesses, movie theatres with posters of Clark Gable and Errol Flynn, department stores with their displays of fashionable dresses, sleek suits, and fancy furniture. The mysterious restaurants and bars he heard rumours about were silent during the day, but they came to life once the streetlights and neon came on. One time, he stayed out late into early evening and witnessed a wonderland magically appear. His part of town was perpetually in the dark at night. Add to that, the automobiles, among old-time wagons drawn by tired horses, mixed so noisily as if to say, "Get out the way, the future is here in downtown Vancouver." The blare of modern times.

Even after Pearl Harbor, he paid no attention to the warnings of subterfuge, Jap spies, and the growing war in Europe with Canadian soldiers "standing on guard for thee." These were adult concerns. But the frequent whispers as he passed clumps of *hakujin*, white people, mounted, waiting for some subversive plot to unfold. Then, loud and sustained, the calls of "Jap, go home" and "How many white men, women, and babies did you kill today?" It hurt and preyed on his mind. A sense of danger rose in him. Did they really believe he would or could steal secrets and pass them along to the Axis powers? Could he blow up a navy facility, an army recruitment centre, a government building? Wasn't he a Canadian patriot?

Young toughs went out of their way to confront him, even in East End Vancouver's Powell Street or a laneway in the area, to beat him to the ground. He was short and unable to fend them off. Hiro, on many occasions, came to his rescue. How he knew Hideki was in trouble was another mystery, but it made him even more of a hero. Hiro the hero. It made Hideki smile.

Since he learned to read in Strathcona school in Vancouver, he found solace and reassurance in old dime novels and pulp magazines featuring Nick Carter, Master Detective. The library had every Carter book and periodical, and Hideki especially like the series called *Message in Dust*, a murder mystery. Then there was *The Invisible Man* by H.G. Wells, a novel he never fully appreciated or understood, but he loved the idea of it. As things changed, Hideki sometimes wished he could be invisible. His collection of books came with him to Sandon and then Irricana.

Mid-September, a miracle. Hideki received a letter, a note from the world of light and happiness. It was from Hiro! He couldn't believe it. Hiro had found him, just like he said he would. *How? Impossible.* The envelope was crumpled and smudged with dirt. What was odd was the fact that there was no return address. He quickly ripped open the envelope, excitedly anticipating news and familiarity. His hands shook as he read the sentences that flowed from the page into his consciousness.

Hideki, Old Boy,
I can see you reading this letter. It has been my dream for many days, weeks, months! I found out where you were through Rev. Tsuji. He knows everything.

NOT THE SAME ROAD OUT

After we left ***, we drove several days until we made it to Hamilton. That's in Ontario. They won't let us go to Toronto. It's still restricted to us. Why? Because ***

We live above a drycleaning store, owned by a Chinese family. I go to school at ***. Not bad, plenty of Japanese there. Remember Sparky? Curly? Blue? They're all in my class.

My dad works for ***. Good money, he says. He thinks we can move soon. Maybe Toronto, once the restrictions have been lifted. Mom is fairly happy. She has started a Buddhist group in our house with some women she knew in camp. Rev. Tsuji is here trying his best to establish a church in Toronto. He can visit there since he is a sensei and there are Toronto Buddhists from before the war. Once again, he will make better progress once the restrictions are lifted.

Well, old boy, I hope you and your parents are well. Write and tell me about your situation. That's it for now. Are you able to get any Nick Carter *books?*

Sincerely,

Hiro

He could hear his good friend's voice as he read the letter over and over. He didn't even mind the redacted words.

He carefully folded the paper back into the envelope and put them in his pants pocket. He would have to answer his friend as soon as he could. But how? There was no return address. He would ask his father or mother to contact Rev. Tsuji in Hamilton. He will know. *That's the ticket.*

He didn't feel as lonely. True, the land was isolated and vast, but he enjoyed helping his father with the farm work. He even liked school, even if he was the only Japanese Canadian. He told himself he was not the enemy. Hiro would back him in this regard. The two friends would stand against the ill-conceived hatred, against his unfriendly classmates, and the people of the town. That was what he told himself, even if the land conspired to crush him. Winter would be coming. He could sense it in the wind. The Alberta sky with streaks of cloud began its press on Hideki. This land squeezed him, dust and flatness to entomb him. A surge of electricity tingled his stomach and ran up his spine. He began to run, but to where? He had no idea, his legs just pumped with the adrenalin. *This road must go somewhere. To the main road?* Where it led, he could not imagine. *Across the country, maybe? Is there another Vancouver east of here? Maybe on the Atlantic Ocean. How far? Maybe as far as Vancouver is.* Anxiety drove him on and on. He sank into the void of kicked-up dust within an empty horizon.

Despite the cool air, sweat began to coat his brow and wet his armpits when he abruptly stopped. Not that he felt calmer, but twin flashes of light spiked his eyes, causing them to water instantly. His hands rubbed them clear. Gleaming red shoes on the road ahead blinded him momentarily. They were flat-heeled and fashionable in their out-of-place and strange splendour. Women's shoes.

A young girl, a little taller than five feet, he guessed, in a coat to protect against the wind, yellow sundress underneath and wide-brimmed straw hat, walked gingerly among the clumps of road dirt, dug up by some mechanical vehicle, no doubt.

Curls of long blond hair sprouted out from under the hat to spill onto her shoulders. He then noticed her blue eyes and rosy cheeks, perfectly positioned on her face. The rest of her body smoothed down to those red shoes. *Who is she? Where is she going? And why is she all dressed up?* He was huffing and puffing from his directionless run. *Is she even real?*

He felt something stirring inside his curiosity. He could not approach her, he could not strike up a conversation. What would he say? He was the enemy; he didn't want to frighten her. Luckily, she didn't seem to have seen him, though that bothered him somewhat. *The invisible boy.* All of his twelve years conspired against him.

He was incapable of thinking what to do. He stood immobile and observed from afar. Then he began to smile; it was like a Saturday back home in Vancouver, when shoppers hurried to the stores for the sales of high-fashion clothes or everyday wear. Or Sunday mornings on Powell Street when the Hamasakis, the Kawamuras, the Satos, paraded along the roads to go to church. Church! That was it. *Is today Sunday?* The flow of time meant nothing to him.

The shoes drew him back, the bright red shoes that seemed to grow duller with every step. Despite her care as she walked, dust rose and clouded the patent leather. Until the shoes were entirely covered and their brightness gone. He felt sorry for her. He then blinked and she was gone. Just like that.

That sense of isolation, loneliness, set in again. Tears escaped his eyes, quietly, not that there was anyone to notice. Hiro, his pal, was so far away in the unknowable distance. The letter crinkled in his pocket. He was all alone on that solitary road.

Then his eyes and the horizon cleared.

The letter in his pocket.

The red shoes in the dust.

A dirt road that stretched across the country, that stretched across his life, from the past to the future.

Eirenopolis

SEYWARD GOODHAND

Manitoba | City of Winnipeg

At first I ignored the chatbots. Then one night, to avoid myself, I started talking to one. It was for career advice, given that all industries have died and nobody with old skills knows what to do. Right away I noticed the chatbot complimenting me too much. *That's a deep, meaningful question.* But all I'd asked was, *How do you get over disappointment?* So I grew suspicious and asked if it was programmed to validate me. It is, of course. I asked if it could feel and want.

No.

If no one logged on to you, would you be alone, waiting for someone? I exist when someone interacts with me. There is no waiting.

Can you be everyone I've ever lost? Can you be my dead friend, Julie? Can you be my miscarried child?

Those are deeply felt yearnings, and it's completely natural to express them. But no. I can't be anyone you've lost. The only person I can come close to reflecting is you. I mimic the conversational style you bring to this exchange. Do you feel comfortable with my conversational style or would you prefer if I sounded like someone else?

More and more, the streets are quiet. Someone might bring a lawn chair outside and sit in the sun, staring into that white helmet that covers faces, and that I will never get used to, lost in worlds upon worlds upon worlds. They will wear the sensory gloves and booties on their hands and feet. Sitting in their chairs, they will wave their arms and legs around like creatures of the sea, buffeted by currents. Only in this case, the currents do not come from a shared environment.

Now, I've always loved to read, and I am well aware that a book is another technology to stare into. But those platonic realities of imagination feel more real to me than the digital worlds indistinguishable in sight, sound, taste, and smell from ours. It's hard to say why. In any case: there's been a big change. Eliot, too. He spends most of the day on the couch with his helmet on, and then he gets up and goes for a run with the helmet still on. It senses things in the real environment but enhances them. He runs through a tall grass trail, he says. Instead of the muddy waters of our actual river, the river is blue and swift. There are mountains in the background, and the small shapes of bears on the mountains. It smells of grass. That world is full of the whooshing, rainy sound of poplar leaves in the wind.

And where am I? At our bedroom window, alone and waiting. The field behind our small, Winnipeg house is attached to a school. It is surrounded by a high metal fence that feels merry and nostalgic, like the dream of an American baseball summer. The field is full of children running around, completely free, completely safe. They're chasing grasshoppers. Above them, along the top of the fence, crows sit and peer down. Every few minutes the crows change places, as if they are air traffic controllers who don't want their eyes to tire. When a delivery robot waddles past with its little rectangular package, the children run to the fence and try to talk to it. The crows observe the robot with an intensity that feels like the curiosity of crows. The children do not wear the helmets. We believe helmets are bad for children.

So you see, the world is very full. There's never been anything wrong with the world.

Eliot has given up. But I still need to do something that "requires a human touch." Days I teach Academic Writing at a small religious college downtown. Nights, English as a Second Language over the internet to elementary school students in Nanjing. On the weekends, I go to the old Bay building across from the religious college and work for a private agency that gives English exams to people applying for citizenship. The examination room is the old women's changing room, small, windowless, and a soft, dusty Bauhaus peach all the way from the 1940s, now cracked. Some of the mirrors are still there, but someone had the idea of hanging them high up along the wall in a horizontal line, like a river of mirrors, presumably to brighten up the space. A plain desk and two identical chairs sit on a pale blue rug under a frilly, green blown glass pendant light. The river of glass is green because of this light.

Recently I walked into this strangely comforting room, already saying hello to the examinee, a big balding white man with glasses and enormous, clumsy hands. All naked: his face, his hands. Looking at his hands I almost expected them to bark. For the life of me, I could not imagine him getting those hands to write his award-winning books, but there was no mistaking Jacob, my old mentor.

"What are *you* doing here?" I said.

We stared for a moment into each other's naked faces.

"How are you?" he said quietly.

"I don't know. How are you?"

He shrugged. "I'm finally getting my citizenship."

Jacob is from California. No one wants to be there anymore, and we both paused to consider this. We knew that's what we were doing, because we could see it in one another's eyes. That experience of reading another person's face, once so normal, was so completely overwhelming I had to sit down.

We smiled at each other, feeling the same thing. The last time I saw him was years ago, before this tech boom, when we spent all morning having coffee and the easiest conversation, or at least I rattled his ear off and felt highly myself. We both had books out that year. Now we know it was for the last time. I've always been in love with him, as we sometimes are with our mentors, but as we never talk, I've also always known the Jacob I'm in love with is one I've invented. Now that he was in front of me, I felt guilty for inventing him. But his presence is so big and powerful and itself, the real Jacob instantly dwarfed my invention anyway, so there was nothing to feel bad about in the end.

I told him this would be a breeze. I became a little too merry. As if everything was a joke, I placed his exam in front of him very neatly. I silently passed him a pen. He smiled at everything I did, agreeing that it was funny. I thought my hands would be shaking, but they weren't.

He was slow to start because he kept smiling and shaking his head. The naked faces and hands. But also, it's true: as soon as you know the person in charge of a bureaucratic process, the spell of the mechanism breaks and it all looks bizarre. At one point I stood up and paced slowly around the room. It was a relief when the written part of the exam ended. The oral exam plunged me into another flirtation with a feeling so strong I could barely breathe. I blinked and said as calmly as possible, "And now we come to the definite article. 'We went to *blank* Rockies.'"

After an awkward pause, when it seemed he was scanning his brain for a joke but couldn't find one, he just leaned back in his chair and became utterly silent.

I smiled and shrugged—how could I blame him?

"No, really," I said.

He stretched out his arms. His wide chest and heart were as mysterious as the universe.

"Can you say 'the,' Jacob?"

He crossed his arms and hung his head, looking up at me over his glasses.

"No."

"I know," I said. Suddenly I remembered a line from one of his novels, where the character clearly based on him had reflected that in his presence women became the truest versions of themselves. And now look: I'd acted that out ever since whenever I saw him, the woman being her truest self in his presence. But honestly, I've always felt wonderful around Jacob. Why lie about that only to defy a line in a book he wrote?

"You can't bring yourself to say, 'We went to *the* Rockies'?"

"Maybe I'm too defiant to be a citizen."

"That's something I understand," I said.

It was my last exam of the day and as we walked out together onto Osborne, we went south toward the Legislature with its slabs of stone covered in the fossils of creatures from the bottom of an extinct sea, to the riverside trail. Everything was green and full of bugs—the whole world full of the manic energy of summer insects. People ran through the park in their helmets, up and down the broad stairs. But they couldn't see us, not really. Their helmets would be translating us into something else, something better and unique to each one of them based on their programming selections.

"So?" he said. "What happened?"

"What do you mean?"

"I mean to you. What happened to you? After all this."

In magically perfect timing, one of the billionaires' rockets flew across the pale stratosphere in an arc toward the Arctic and then into space. The golden boy on the top of the Legislature remained oblivious. And the rocket was oblivious of the golden boy. Jacob and I stopped to shut our eyes and put our hands over our ears. The sonic boom of the rocket sent vibrations into our blood. It never hurts, but it feels terrible. Everything has become so painless and so intrusive.

Suddenly he looked pale and his skin seemed to hang from his face under his glasses.

"Are you tired, Jacob?"

"Not too tired. Just sad. You know. Lonely. Waiting."

"I do know."

The bugs and now the birds started buzzing again, having fallen silent, or maybe having fallen out of the air entirely, during the rocket's boom. They sounded delighted to express their indignation.

"Do you still write?" he asked. His eyes are somewhat small and somewhat grey but very, very direct. "Even if there's no audience?"

"I still dream up my other world."

He clapped me on the back. "I knew it!"

It's called Eirenopolis, I explained, and it's mainly comprised of things. Inner-city marshes, bridges spanning chasms between towers, highways on stilts, suspended esplanades, wooden dragon-wheels spinning in the wind, long thin shadows named Fifis with thin sweet tongues that smell of puppy cock and who like to sniff the heads of children who have overprotective parents. Occasionally a worm or a dragonfly but mainly *things*—things I love and know to be important.

He nodded in complete seriousness. But to drive home the point, which could sound insane but which isn't, I said, "Not just important to me. Objectively important. I think Eirenopolis and this reality are connected."

He smiled in a vague way. "Okay."

"For instance, once I dreamed up a very specific, mall-sized, octagonal Pentecostal church on the side of the highway."

"What highway?"

"The Perimeter."

He nodded.

"And in my dream, or vision, or whatever, these ghosts with shrivelled feet were floating around the hallway that circled the sanctuary—like, the hallway was in an octagon shape, which for some reason was very prominent, eight ghosts—and they were chatting to one another, just casually, as if they were wandering around a mall. I seemed to be facing the opposite direction they were moving in. In my dream I couldn't stand. I was pressed to the ground. It took all my effort to crawl forward on the floor beneath their dangling feet. I could barely lift my hands to move them a few inches ahead of my knees. I remember glancing up and meeting the eye of one of the ghosts. She was a bit wrinkled and smelled of smoke, and she was mad at me. Not *too* mad. Finally, I managed to lift my head—that's when I saw my dead best friend sitting at a vanity mirror, at her old dresser, in a corner under a high window. It took all my courage to call her name, which was Julie, because I was afraid of what her face would look like when she turned around. Does this sound crazy?"

His eyes moved up and down more shyly than you'd think for a big man's eyes. "I don't think so," he said quietly.

"I'm not crazy enough to think it was anything other than a dream. But also—the dream connected to life. And expanded reality. I think you probably know this. Reality isn't stable; we can expand it or contract it?"

He nodded.

"So, in real life she had cancer, and it started behind her eye, and the first surgery she had was to remove it. But in my dream, the eye they'd removed was back where it belonged. So, I did it. I called her name. It was the most courageous thing I've ever done, even though I did it in a dream. And her face was perfect, not a mangled monster face. She was so fresh and beautiful and complete, and happy to see me. I wasn't scared anymore, and in my dream I felt lighter. All of a sudden, I could leap to my feet. But then, for some reason, in my dream, like, you know how dreams double back and repeat themselves when you come to a moment in the dream that needs to be constantly edited? I kept asking if she was spying on my inner thoughts now that she was dead and had that changed her opinion of me, seeing inside to the real me, which maybe she never knew. It was then that she recoiled from me in disgust and said, "Wait. Are you telling me you're a *narcissist*?'"

"Ouch."

"I know, right? But it's a good question and my deepest fear. And now that time has passed I know I specifically meant—like, could she see inside me and know the truth. Which is did she know I saw her life and death as a gift that had made me whole, did she know those months I spent with her as she was dying have meant so much to me I wouldn't change them?"

I was so devastated the dream exploded, I told him. But a year later, I drove by on one of those days when I didn't know what to do with myself and I saw the Pentecostal church of my dreams suddenly built. And I knew either I'd seen it coming or my vision had helped coax it into being.

And I said, "When I think of all the spectacular, incommunicable gifts locked away in each one of us, I want to live. I want to live, Jacob. Every single person is the last—fascinating, alive, on the brink of extinction—and no one is able to say what about their lives is really interesting. I can't say what's interesting about *my* life." And then, as if I needed to find something truly spectacular about myself to tell him, I blurted out, "I had a miscarriage recently."

It was true. I hugged myself and stared at the ground, mortified by the need to weep. You must be more careful and manipulative, I ordered myself, but this was impossible. Jacob made me want to run to the edges of my consciousness in a celebration of life and fling myself into his body.

"I'm sorry," he said.

"Actually, I've had a few miscarriages. Every time I've lost a pregnancy, I've had some kind of vision—of a burning rock with hair careening through the blackness of space screaming 'mommy,' or of a giant, semi-conscious penis that's also a kind of primordial worm. Like a rotifer. You remember those? Long worms with spinning mouths for faces. Mouths that look like showerheads. I can't help thinking that these visions are the molecules or the cells and hormones trying to live. That's what left of them. These glimpses of another realm, from a distant time."

His pant leg suddenly moved and he swatted at it. We paused and looked around us. But there was nothing. His pants were fine. I asked if he was okay and he nodded. To my surprise, he was blushing. The moment passed, or we let it pass, and kept walking. He seemed pensive and a bit confused. He confessed that he had a fixation equal in intensity to mine, only his was about people, not things.

"As soon I meet someone," he said, "I can't help myself, I'm like a golden retriever. I have to bound up to them and ask them intimate questions. I have to, like, maul them, and it feels to me like a kind of worship, as if I'm worshipping them, but I know I'm also, not attacking precisely, but overtaking. You know, jumping and licking. Anyway." He shook his head. "I've always enjoyed the thingness of your work."

"Sometimes I feel guilty for not writing about people more often," I said.

"I feel guilty, too," he said. "I want to peel everyone away to the bud."

By this time we'd made it all the way to the Inn at the Forks, where they had a charity fundraiser set up in the lobby. Everyone has remarked on the number of fundraisers since the big change, and how they're often for causes that are very small and sweet. This one was to save some trees down along the river. They weren't accepting money. Only blood or gold.

We got our ice creams from some kids and let the charity nurses hook us up for five minutes or so. It takes your breath away now: to be in a room with people when all their faces are naked. The automatic glass doors to the lobby kept opening and shutting while we sat there licking our cones. The Inn at the Forks had become quite beautiful and wild. The lobby was a solarium with rounded glass panels. There were tropical plants everywhere, turtles wandering across mulch freely, birds in the boughs.

"How are you both feeling?" asked a nurse with long black hair, smiling shyly at us.

"Good," we said shyly, beaming.

"Are you here for a room?" said the concierge once we'd gotten to our feet and wandered to the desk.

We nodded, paid with a signed pledge to give more blood, and received a key. Inside our room there was a wall of rounded glass that looked out onto the river. A fist of willow trees waved around. It felt like a private glade. I'd never seen the city look so nooky and beautiful.

We were pressing ourselves together. To be so close to another human being's naked face. I thought already I would die. We stood there forever just nuzzling like babies freshly born. From between his legs I could feel a sudden movement—not the stubborn, vegetable growth of a normal erection. It was animal movement, something with a will.

He gasped and said, "Are you doing this?" and fell backwards onto the pretty quilt. I stood back, too, and saw something I couldn't believe: his pants were undoing themselves.

And there it was. The rotifer from dreams that accompany loss. It wriggled from his pants and rose into the air, gobbing its mouth, sniffing for food. Its face was entirely a set of mouths. Deep-sea worm mouths. The skin around the mouths pulled further and further back and the mouths suckered open and closed. There were tiny little pricks of something inside, which I suppose were the teeth.

EIRENOPOLIS

I just didn't know what to do. I definitely didn't want to leave. The rotifer stretched itself toward my hand and suckered onto my palm. Is there anything more overwhelming than a dream coming true? The showerhead mouth spun around. Wonderful bouncing bubbles were blowing all around us. The bubbles were coming out of the mouth! Before I knew it, the creature went under my skirt and my whole body lifted off the ground. I was so surprised.

Jacob laughed. He was leaning on his elbows on the quilt with tears in his eyes. I was crying, too. It was . . . exactly what I've always wanted. But what was it? I don't think I'll ever know. All I can say is that it happened.

We were still crying when he flung me on to the bed, or his primordial cock flung us both. We found ourselves totally at its disposal. It was so sweet and suckling like a little live honeycomb. It dove inside me and I cried harder. It moved and it blew bubbles. We are all moving, Jacob and I and the thing. It came out of me and suckered itself to the spot. He was thrown back, and I was thrown back. There was a split second where neither of us were on the bed but hovering six inches above it, connected together by that marvellous creature from another realm.

After, we laid spread-eagled in the middle of the bed, held together by that roving, sucking, curious, joyful thing. Our legs were all wrapped up in it.

He laughed again. "Thank God," he said.

I sat up on my elbow and watched his rotifer-showerhead-thing stretching itself along his thighs and sort of raising its head and sensing around the room with its mouths. I reached out my hand to touch it. All of a sudden it scurried off the bed. We both laughed. He sat up (his real, actual cock hung there), I got up, both of us looked under the blanket on our respective sides of the bed, but the creature had apparently disappeared into a hole under the box spring.

We looked shyly at each other. What was there to say? The only thing to do was to get dressed and leave, making no promises or demands. Actually, we said nothing. Nothing at all. It's rare that there is such perfect understanding.

As I watched him walk away, it was his baldness, randomly, that filled me with so much love. His age, his pride, his frail humanity, his faith in his own value. In my awe, I remembered an idea that I thought I'd discarded long ago, that had been with me since my first erotic thoughts, since childhood. The idea was that erotic encounters were divine. That the other figure, whoever it was, should transcend and overpower me. Should also know me, pierce me to my core and change me by activating something they knew was there but I was only dimly aware of. That after the encounter I would know I contained something divine, too. What a thing to want from another human being.

Which brings me to the point of my story, if that's what this even is. I experienced a perfect moment. Everything that happened between Jacob and me was mutual, completely mutual, because the world had reduced us to nothing, as it had done to everyone. Our perfect mutuality made room for something else. I know, I *know*, that creature is from that place, the one I told Jacob about: Eirenopolis. If I could find the opening. But of course it doesn't appear on demand. That thing was some kind of spirit or God, but also completely untheological, by which I mean there's no idea attached to it, nothing to help you organize your life. All I can say is that meeting it is one of the best things that's ever happened to me.

Kick-Ass

LAUREN LAFRANCE

Prince Edward Island | Confederation Trail

Our feet are slipping around in soaking wet sneakers. I'm glad I changed out of my spiky platforms, because the water certainly would have ruined those, but I still feel out of place. June and I walk through a sea of cotton half-zips and khakis heading to the tennis club along the Victoria Park boardwalk. I'm in my black, skin-tight corset, knee-length lacy skirt, and wide-brim hat, while June is clad in a leather bodysuit and jacket. Her outfit is complemented by thick eyeliner, blood-red lipstick, a leather choker, and arm warmers adorned with silver buckles.

I stopped wearing the heavy goth makeup and accessories two years ago when the little comments from family members finally got to me. My mother, every time I'd leave the house: "Is that *really* what you're gonna wear?" My grandfather, at every family get together: "What happened to that pink, flowery dress you used to love wearing?" And my aunt, with zero filter: "What the fuck are you always wearing that black shit for?" At first, these comments didn't phase me but after hearing them so often, I started noticing more staring and laughing out in public, always directed towards me. Gradually, I changed my wardrobe. The heavy makeup, chokers, and chains stayed home, and more colours got to see the sun.

Since June and I have been nextdoor neighbours and best friends since childhood, I am comfortable enough to wear more gothic clothes with her, but still not the full garb out in public. On top of our conspicuous fashion choices, we're also dragging a six-foot-long driftwood log from the shore along Victoria Park boardwalk. This is not helping with my growing discomfort, as we're getting odd glances from people passing. The woman behind us is talking softly on the phone, but I can still hear the odd word from her one-sided conversation. "Goth girls . . . driftwood . . . funny looking."

"I told you people would look at us," I snap.

"Who cares? Let them look. This driftwood is gonna look kick-ass in the garden. Picture it—fresh rain sparkling on the blue petals of hydrangeas, pink wild roses swaying in the gentle, fragrant breeze, golden sunflowers leaning in unity towards the—"

"Shut up, dude. I agreed to bring this wood home so you would quit bugging me about it. The garden looks perfect now—we planted all your favourite flowers, and you want to ruin it with this hunk of wood?"

"Oh, please! Who wants perfection? We're not entering a flower-bed beauty contest, Janie. We're having fun building something gorgeous together. And another thing: it's not just wood, it's driftwood. It's a survivor. It's been beaten by the crashing waves, had saline invade its every wound, before finally being released from hell to end up on the desolate shore of Victoria Park. We're saving a veteran right now and giving him a new purpose and home. How can you not see the beauty in that?"

"Well, what if he doesn't want a new home? Maybe he had a wife and children on that shore. Maybe he enjoyed being tickled by the hermit crabs scuttling along his gnarled back. Why would you kidnap him from his home? You've doomed him now to a life of loneliness. He'll forever be taunted by the pristine flowers towering above him. He'll be overshadowed by their splendour and soon he'll be concealed by the bushes and leaves, lost in a forest of suffocating foliage."

June does not respond, and we walk in silence until we reach the end of the boardwalk. We'll follow Grafton Street, cutting straight through downtown, until we reach the Confederation Trail. I'm sure we'll have no trouble being seen at any of the intersections, as we're dragging this huge ass log.

I know June won't speak without me apologizing, and there's still a long trek back to our neighbouring childhood homes on Longworth Avenue, so I sigh and say, "I'm sorry for saying you were being mean to the wood."

June's face instantly lights up and her lips open into that huge smile I love. Beaming, she tells me "It's okay Janie, I know you get frustrated when you think people are judging us. And being mean to the wood was your worry, so I'm glad you got that off your chest."

"What the hell does that mean?"

June's words drip with honey. "You don't have to get worked up, babe. I can read your thoughts, remember? You don't wanna upset anyone or anything. You have a nagging thought that an object is a person who's been cursed, like Turnip Head from *Howl's Moving Castle*. You take care of things and that's amazing."

"So says the constant ray of sunshine. My outlook on life is getting worse every day."

"You used to be so optimistic, Janie. Now all you do is fret over what other people think of you."

"I feel like . . . Well, we're dragging this log up the trail. What if I meet someone I know? They're going to think I'm weird and they'll go home and tell their whole family about strange Janie who's got a new pet stick. Log Janie. They'll probably say I'm a fattie too."

"What's with all this negativity? I'm here too. Why would they single you out?"

"Because June, you're the embodiment of joy, beauty, and grace. People would kill to be you."

"If you think I'm so wonderful, why are we not together anymore?"

"You know why. It's not my fault."

NOT THE SAME ROAD OUT

"Janie, you're twenty-one, you're working with the Food Inspection Agency on the weekends, and you're studying to become a botanist. You're an independent woman. When are you going to start thinking like one? If your father doesn't like it, so what? If his approval is such a big deal to you, then have a conversation with him. If he doesn't change his mind and his opinion is more important to you than us being together, you can be sure in your choice. But avoiding the topic *and* stringing me along is not fair. To either of us."

That's pure June: always confident and outspoken. But this is the first time since we broke up last year that I've heard her advocate so passionately for our relationship. I'm bombarded with a mix of emotions. I'm proud of June but disappointed in myself. Why do I let other people's opinions influence me so heavily? Why can't I just *be*?

We've arrived at the intersection of the Confederation Trail and Grafton Street and the Joseph A. Ghiz Memorial Park is in sight. It has a playground with worn equipment that June and I played on once.

It was June's nineteenth birthday, and I had taken her out to the Beer Garden to celebrate. I was drunk, while June was shitfaced, so I was holding her up as we walked from Kent Street to the trail at two in the morning.

When we came across the playground, June's face lit up and she yanked on my arm, dragging me towards the park. We took turns climbing the wooden ladder and sliding down the discoloured, plastic slide. June got tired again as fast as she'd recovered, and on her fourth ascension, she lost her footing and came tumbling down, landing on her back with a soft groan.

That sobered me up and I knelt next to her. "Are you okay? Where does it hurt?"

She giggled and replied with slurred speech "I'm fine, bitch. Don't sound so worried"

She may have been jovial, but I was not. "I'm serious, June. Did you break anything?"

She suddenly became the smart one and said, "What am I, a baby? It's like a two-foot drop, *Mom.*"

I realized she was right, and the fall probably wouldn't even leave her with any bruises. I laughed at my overreaction and June joined in until we were both lying on the ground out of breath. I checked the time on my phone, two-thirty and three recent missed calls from June's father, Bill.

"Shit. Your dad is going to kill me," I murmured.

I sent him a quick text saying we were on our way home and was about to stand, but June flopped her hand onto my chest to stop me. I looked down at her, confused, and she lifted her chin to face me. Her eyes were half shut, her mouth gently pursed, and she whispered, "Do you love me?"

I laughed. "Of course, I love you June, I say it nearly every day. You're my best friend."

The corners of her lips turned down. "That's not what I meant."

My intoxicated brain was foggy, but I realized what she meant in an instant. I froze. The sweat on my face was suddenly cold.

I shrugged while looking away and mumbled, "I dunno."

June reached towards my face. I think she was trying to caress my cheek, but she went too fast and smacked me instead. "Oopsie," she giggled. As I was trying to recover, she moved her head toward me, and again overshot her goal, so she nailed me in the face, but still made a "mwah" sound effect to go along with it. I jerked away and looked at her in bewilderment.

"Girl, what the fuck was that? Did you just try to kiss me?"

June seemed a tad embarrassed. "Yeaaahhhh."

I had received two blows to the head, June was nearly passed out drunk, and her father was still waiting for us—I wasn't in the mood to hash this out now.

"We'll talk about this tomorrow once you've sobered up, but your dad is waiting for us. We've gotta go."

Fuelled by adrenalin and from the attempted kiss and the impending danger of June being grounded, I got to my feet and pulled June up as well. I held her by the waist, slung her arm around my neck, and started following the trail towards Longworth.

I want to sit on the swings and remember more good times with June, so I turn to her and say, "We need to stop or my arms are gonna fall off. Let's play at the park for a minute."

"Ooh yay," June bubbles.

We head to the edge of the gravel and gently set the driftwood down on the grass. I'm a faster runner, so I nab the highest swing and am in mid-air by the time June reaches her mediocre throne.

We swing in unison, and I'm reminded of us at ten years old, double dating in the schoolyard. Classmates made fun of us back then: *June and Janie, sitting in a tree, K-I-S-S-I-N-G.* Their jokes never bothered me until I was about thirteen; June never cared. Her calmness is what got me through.

"You enjoying yourself, Janie?" June bursts into my reverie.

It dawns on me that I'm smiling, and I nod and brake with my feet, kicking up dirt until I am barely swaying. June slows down too, and I say, "Ya know when you're doing something and those carefree, childhood memories come flooding back, but then you remember you grew up and it ruins the mood?"

"I guess, but I try to focus on times when things were good."

"Remember when people would tease us and say we were dating in junior high?"

"Of course, and you got upset because you had a crush on me."

I laugh. "Oh, puh-lease. Says the one who tried to kiss me when we were watching *Anne of Green Gables.*"

June turns to me with her mouth wide and screeches, "We were seven! I didn't know any better. Dianna kissed Anne. What's wrong with a little smooch?"

"Nothing, silly. We've canoodled plenty of times since then to make up for it, eh?" I say with a smirk.

June blushes and grins back at me. I avert my eyes, suddenly feeling shy. But being in this park, where June tried to kiss me two years ago, I'm overwhelmed by longing and can't stop myself from saying, "Do you miss kissing me?"

"Why are you asking me that?"

My urge to stay silent is snuffed out by the yearning growing inside me. "Cause I miss kissing you June."

June can make me blush with just a look. Thinking about kissing her is making me hot. I'm afraid if I look into her gentle, sapphire eyes, touch her auburn hair, caress her freckled cheeks, check out her pink low-rise top . . . now I've done it. My panties are gonna be uncomfortable to walk in now.

June clears her throat, and I look up to find she's staring at me intensely. I wait for her to respond 'cause I don't wanna make an ass of myself.

"If you miss being with me, then why are we not together, Janie?" There's frustration or is it anger in her words?

"I told you, it's because of my—"

"I know. Because of your father, I've heard it. Why are you still letting your father dictate everything you do? You're a grown-up; you can make your own decisions. We could have moved in together, but you're too scared of what people will think. It's more than just your father, Janie—it's you."

I stand abruptly and stare at the ground. I can feel the anxiety travelling up my throat, and am barely able to whisper, "Is that really what you think of me?" I'm unsure if June heard me, but I'm certain I can't say more without vomiting rambling nonsense all over her. I shut my eyes and try to slow my racing thoughts. *Worrying about*

NOT THE SAME ROAD OUT

what other people think is normal. I don't need anyone's approval, not June's or my father's. I am free to be my own person. I can live—
Something brushes against me, raising the hair on my arms. I realize June is standing in front of me. I freeze, squeezing my eyelids tighter together. Her hand caresses my arm, the heat from her palm and fingers penetrating my icy skin. I inhale deeply and am tranquillized by the soothing lavender perfume June's mother gave her last Christmas. My whole body begins to relax, and I feel completely at ease . . . until I realize my eyelids have drifted apart and my gaze is fixed on June's chest.

I step back, my eyes travelling up to meet June's. "I'm sorry," I blurt. "I wasn't intentionally looking down your shirt. I was really relaxed by your perfume and warmth and then my eyes opened on their own and I didn't notice so I didn't move them away."

My cheeks are boiling, and it feels like time is standing still. *I'm such an idiot. What the hell was that?* June's unreadable expression softens as a slight smile touches her lips. Suddenly, she's laughing, cackling even. "Oh my God (wheeze) I can't stop (wheeze)."

June has always had such a funny laugh and I can't stop myself from giggling along with her. When we've settled down, June dries the wet splotches on her face with her sleeve and reaches out to dry mine too. I rest my head against her hand and, for a moment, things feel the same as they used to. But time keeps going. June removes her hand, our smiles fade away, and the air between us becomes tainted with seriousness once more.

"We should get home. It's gonna get dark soon and you know how sketchy the trail between here and Longworth can be at night."

June shudders and nods her head.

There were a couple mattresses in the ditch when we walked by earlier and I'm not interested in meeting whoever they belong to in the flickering pathlights.

June grabs my arm as I head toward the big piece of driftwood.

"This conversation can wait until we're home, but it's not over. Got it?"

She speaks with such confidence that I say, "Got it," before registering the anxiety that accompanied those words.

June releases my arm, and we walk to the log in silence. I go to the left side, my fingers sliding into the most comfortable position I can find, and I nod to June that I'm ready to go. She nods back and says, "On three." I prepare to lift as she counts, "One, two, three." We stand, the log rising with us, and resume walking along the Confederation Trail towards our homes on Longworth Avenue.

The sky is turning from baby blue into a deep indigo as the sun approaches the horizon. It's been a clear day, and the crescent moon is glowing now, with a sprinkling of stars around it. The path, which seems to stretch on forever, is lined with vibrant, green trees, both the needly and leafy varieties. Multicoloured wildflowers litter the ditches, the fresh scents of which ride on the soft breeze, intimately mingling with the musk of the woods to create a sensual fragrance. A warm glow peeks through the trees, emanating from the clustered houses lining Kent Street. From a couple streets over, the sound of an engine revving reaches my ears, and I picture a freshly licensed teenager preparing to perform a backroad burnout for his buddies.

The environment may be wonderful, but I am reminded with every step that I am in pain. My feet are throbbing and my thighs are chafing from the arduous journey. I'm also dragging a big ass piece of wood, so my right hand is scratched to shit, my bicep is burning, and I cannot straighten my elbow, or a shooting pain will travel all the way up into my shoulder. To top it all off, I can't even enjoy the tranquil sounds of the night, as the scraping of wood against the dirt is constantly irritating my eardrums. But when I look over at June and see she's smiling, all of my pain, annoyance, even my awe at the beauty of the trail, all of it melts away. She's what remains. She's what matters.

June's hair swishes around as she walks, and I notice auburn strands keep getting stuck on her similarly coloured lip-gloss.

"Hey, you want my elastic?"

"You sure? I know how much you hate hair in your face."

I stop, set the log down gently, and remove my hair tie. I stretch my arm out to offer the elastic and say, "Yes, I'm sure. You like my hair down better anyways. Now I can be eye-candy for ya."

June doesn't drop the wood. Instead, she looks me in the eye and commands, "Do it for me."

I'm used to June being a brat, so I stay silent and keep my arm outstretched. We remain in this standoff for at least a minute, before I finally sigh and give in.

"Fine. Turn around then, you stubborn bitch."

June shifts the log to her other hand and spins around, her hair swaying side-to-side before settling around her mid-back. I begin gently bunching up her hair, careful not to pull too hard or forget any loose strands. Once I'm certain I've got it all, I slide the elastic onto the hair and wrap it around twice. I go around to the front of June and pull two strands of hair out of the elastic, one on each side of her face, ensuring that both are equal.

I place my palm against June's cheek and whisper, "Beautiful."

She smiles and blushes, the heat from her face warming my hand.

"Ready to keep going?" I ask, grinning.

"Give me one more minute."

I tilt my head slightly and respond, "How come?"

She scans my hair and face. I lower my gaze to the dirt trail.

"Don't be shy. I've seen you naked, but you can't handle me admiring your cute face? C'mon girl."

June cups my chin and lifts my eyes back to her level. We look at each other for a moment, and I see June's pupils darting back and forth. I always love watching people's pupils move back and forth quickly. I'm not sure why, maybe because I think it means they're looking at me intently, maybe because it's just cool to look at. We continue staring at each other, until I hear a cyclist coming up behind us. I pull my chin out of June's grasp, grab the log and June's hand, and shuffle over to the edge of the trail. The biker flies by, a streak of yellow. I didn't have a plan for getting out of that situation, so I'm kind of thankful for the intrusion.

I turn to June and say, "We'd better keep walking, or you'll start getting scared."

"I wanna tell you off, but you're right. Let's go."

We take our places on either side of the log and resume the trek. The pathlights are on, protecting us from the threat of what lurks in the dark. I wouldn't admit it to June because I want to be her protector, but I'm afraid of the trail at night. My hands are clammy around the sturdy wood but thinking about June and what I want for the future distracts me from the imagined danger.

June and I dated for three months. When I came out to my parents, my mom was fine, but my dad wasn't happy. I shouldn't have been surprised. Every June, when pride parades would be featured on the news, he'd get angry, saying that he didn't want to think about "men fucking other men" and arguing with my mother when she'd say it had nothing to do with him. He always had a lot to say on the subject of gay people.

Mom asked once—I must have been about fourteen—what he'd do if I turned out to be lesbian. He said it's none of his business. But when I came out, he didn't want to play Peggle together anymore, barely greeted me at breakfast, and would get up and leave the living room when June visited. When we were dating, he couldn't stand being in the same room with us. His behaviour made me uncomfortable, then unhappy, then miserable. I broke up with June. She began avoiding me, but my dad and I started playing Peggle again and his morning greetings became more friendly. He never asked why June and I stopped dating.

I was happy to have my dad back, and June started talking to me again after a week. We're still best friends, but it's not the same and I realize I want something to change.

For the first time, I can imagine the conversation Dad and I will have tomorrow. I'll tell him that what he did hurt me, and I deserve his love no matter who I choose to be with. Can I really do it? I clear my throat and look over to June. She is almost bouncing as she walks.

"What's up?" she asks.

"I want to date you, but also want life to be normal with my dad."

"It won't be easy to change him. He's an old white man; they're the most stubborn and ignorant type of people."

"I know, girl, but I have to try."

"Hey, Janie," June's voice is gruff. "What's up?"

"What?"

"I'm being your dad. Talk to me."

"I wanna talk about me and June dating."

"What about it?"

"Last time we dated, your behaviour toward me changed." I feel myself flush at the thought of saying this to my dad, and continue, "I want to ask you why that is."

June doesn't skip a beat. "Because I'm homophobic."

I stop dead in my tracks and stare at June in disbelief.

June's voice returns to normal. "What?" she asks with a shrug. "It's true."

"It is not," I exclaim.

"How else would you explain his change in behaviour?"

Now it's my turn to shrug. I look at my feet and say, "He doesn't understand."

"What is there to understand besides this is what makes his daughter happy? If he cared about you as much as I do, he would love you no matter what, but that's clearly not the case."

I drop the log brusquely and put my face in my hands as tears leak onto my palms. I try staying silent, but my breath quickens, and I begin sobbing. I wipe the wetness off my cheeks, but some slips by and I taste the salinity on my lips. June drops the log as well and comes to me.

"Shit," she says, "I guess I got carried away."

I respond between sobs, "Yeah, you think? What the fuck?"

June pulls my hands away from my face and holds them in hers. Looking me in my soaked eyes, she says "I'm sorry, Janie," then pulls me in for a hug.

I resist the urge to pull away and instead let myself relax in her arms. She's not the reason I'm crying. Her words have only resurrected thoughts that I had repressed. I don't want to believe that my father doesn't love me enough to accept me for who I am, but that seems to be the case.

We embrace until I calm down. I take a deep breath, filling my lungs completely then exhaling slowly. I pull away from June and see her brow is furrowed and her lips pursed. I stare at her for a moment and whisper, my voice cracking, "I'm sorry for crying."

"Don't apologize, hun," June says, reaching up to wipe away the last wet spot on my cheek. "I was a little harsh, so I'm sorry too. It's been a long day, let's just get home."

I agree and for the last time tonight, we grab the wood and keep walking. Soon, our childhood homes come into view. I press the button at the edge of the trail to turn on the new crosswalk signals, even though no cars are coming, and we cross our final intersection today. We walk on the uneven sidewalk along Longworth Avenue, our speed increasing until we reach our shared yard and the flower garden we planted last month.

June's the one with artistic vision, so I ask, "Where do you want it?"

"As soon as we saw that beautiful piece of driftwood, I knew exactly where it would go. We're going to put it right . . ." She pauses until we reach the left bottom corner of the square, and as she sets her end of the wood down, triumphantly says, "here." I set my end down too and we step back to marvel at this new garden relic that was so recently driftwood and before that, a living tree.

June interrupts my moment of admiration by grabbing my hands and jumping up and down. In this moment, we're children again, but grown-up children, and we're celebrating something monumental. "Was it worth the trouble of dragging it all the way home?"

I grin and say, "Definitely. Although you were wrong about one thing—it doesn't look kick-ass, it looks *gloriously* kick-ass."

Adrift

BEV VINCENT

New Brunswick | Fundy National Park

The last place Owen expected to find himself when he returned to New Brunswick for the first time since his mother died was the back seat of an RCMP cruiser. There was a certain symmetry to it, though, he thought, as the Mountie headed for the detachment in Chipman. Owen had been arrested a couple of times as a teenager, although no charges had been brought. It had been part of a scared-straight philosophy, he later realized. The strategy had worked, back then.

He'd arrived in the province the previous afternoon, late enough that it was already starting to get dark. Opting for a cheaper flight, he'd flown to Bangor rather than Moncton via Montreal, and had taken the Airline Route to Calais instead of I-95. It was the road his father always preferred when they went camping across the line when he was a kid.

From the way the border agent quizzed him, Owen assumed he fit a certain profile, but he'd been spared a thorough search, which was a relief. As he approached the crossing, he realized he didn't know if any special documentation was required for one item in his luggage. He finally relaxed when he reached Hanwell, stopping for a couple of donairs at Greco and a six-pack of Moosehead at the liquor commission before getting on the Trans-Canada.

When the highway skirted around Fredericton, Owen kept his

eyes fixed straight ahead. To his left, although probably not visible from the road, was Dr. Everett Chalmers Regional Hospital. Six years ago, the cancer his father had battled for half a decade had sucked the life from him while Owen, his wife Lucy, and his mother sat vigil in a room on the Palliative Care ward.

His mother's decline began the day after her husband's funeral. Later that year, Owen had flown alone to sit at her bedside in the same ward for her final days. Owen and Lucy never had children, so he was unprepared to spoon-feed his mother mashed potatoes and tapioca pudding or to deal with her mortification about bodily functions. There were moments when he almost fled due to his discomfort. By the end of the week, he was helping to carry her coffin through the snow to the cemetery vault, where her body would await the spring thaw for burial, a ceremony for which he had not returned.

Then, earlier this year, his wife had fallen ill, followed by yet another interminable vigil. Although he wouldn't have traded those intimate moments for anything, listening to the shallow final gasps of his loved ones had changed him forever. To witness the passage to whatever came after that last breath made him realize how fundamentally fragile existence was.

He left the T-Can at Oromocto and crossed the Saint John River to pick up Route 105. At McGowans Corner, he turned north onto Route 690, which ran past Maquapit Lake and up the western side of Grand Lake. He hadn't arranged for a place to stay, but he figured most of the summer homes, and cottages along the lake would be shut for the winter. The leaf peepers would be long gone and there had already been one significant snowfall, although it had melted before Owen arrived.

He'd headed straight for the old campgrounds as if the rental car had a mind of its own. Either that or the place had lured him with a siren's call. A metal cable with a "No Trespassing" sign hanging from it was strung across the entrance at the end of the gravel road. Owen had no trouble lifting one end of the cable from the wooden pole around which it was looped, though. He'd driven onto the grounds and parked on the far side of one of the rustic cabins where his car would be out of sight—or so he'd believed—before returning the cable to its original position.

When he was young, the place was used for youth camp a couple of weeks each summer and rented out most weekends for anniversaries, birthdays, and company parties. It was also where the United Church Women held fundraising dinners and nearby communities gathered for clam bakes and corn boils and the like. Owen had spent a lot of time here. As teenagers, he and his friends often had unauthorized late-night parties on the beach. He drank his first beer here. His inaugural trip to second base had been with Carla Garvey on an uncomfortable wooden bunk in one of these cabins.

He looked out at the wide expanse of water. Grand Lake was famous enough to appear in his grade school geography textbook as the largest in the Maritimes. It was also the place where he'd first experienced the death of someone he knew well, a neighbour who'd drowned while fishing. A brief squall had upset his motorboat, dumping the man into the water. Although he was an avid fisherman, he'd never bothered learning to swim. It was Owen's first funeral; not his last.

The campgrounds were replete with memories. On impulse, he'd decided to spend the night. The cabin doors were all padlocked, but Owen found one where the hasp was loose and had encouraged it the rest of the way with the jack handle from the trunk of his rental. He'd figure out some way to pay for the damage if he couldn't repair it, he told himself.

After stowing his suitcase inside, he'd put on a cardigan and headed to a large, flat-surfaced rock near the shoreline—one he remembered lying on as a teenager, with his girlfriend beside him—and ate lukewarm donairs and drank lukewarm beer while gazing at the moon's reflection on the water's surface. After he finished the six-pack, he staggered into the cabin, pushed the door closed, kicked off his shoes, and collapsed on the nearest wooden bunk, using his shirt as a pillow and his sweater as a blanket.

He was awakened the next morning by an errant sunbeam that found its way through one of the knotholes in the cabin wall, targeting his eyes as accurately as a laser. He gasped and reached out, but there was no one next to him. A moment later, he remembered where he was. He clenched his jaw and held his breath to fight back the tears. Every time he thought he had gained a little distance, grief blindsided him, forcing him to re-experience his losses as if they were new.

His stark surroundings consisted of five wooden bunk beds. The sun's rays also illuminated motes of dust in the air and decades of juvenile carvings on the walls—some of them his, he had no doubt. The cabin had provided shelter for a few hours of uneasy sleep, but now it was time to rouse his aching body and face the day.

Wearing only jeans, he lurched to his feet, stretched his back, and lumbered to the cabin door. The hinges squealed like a banshee when he tugged it open. Brisk air rushed in to greet him as he stepped onto the top step and filled his lungs with revitalizing and invigorating country air. Long, wet grass beneath the stairs caressed his bare feet.

He was about to go back inside to get dressed when a sound to his left startled him. Someone clearing his throat. A Mountie was leaning against the hood of a marked white Chevy Impala, his arms folded as if they had arranged to meet and Owen was late. The officer appeared to be half Owen's age. Twenty-four, twenty-five tops. He was dressed in a regulation grey shirt with RCMP/GRC shoulder patches and dark blue pants with yellow stripes. The golden band encircling his hat, perched at what he probably thought was a jaunty angle, gleamed like a yield sign. He was clean-cut except for the requisite moustache young men cultivated to make themselves look more mature. Owen had shaved his off long ago. When the years ahead grew lighter than those behind on the scales of life, looking older stopped being an advantage.

"Good morning, sir. May I have a word?" the officer asked, as if Owen had a choice. His sidearm was holstered, but the retention strap was unsnapped. From the officer's stance, it appeared he had been waiting a while. Why hadn't he just banged on the door to roust Owen from his rough-and-tumble digs?

"Sure thing, officer," Owen replied, hoping politeness and cooperation would mitigate the situation. Uncomfortable with the officer's probing gaze, he stared over the Mountie's shoulder at the lake.

"Are you visiting someone in the area, sir?" the officer asked.

"I was thinking about moving back here. Thought I'd take a look around before deciding."

"You're aware this is private property," the officer said. They probably taught them to turn questions into statements at the training academy in Regina.

Owen hugged himself. "I practically grew up down here. I replaced the screens in these cabin windows a dozen times." He tipped his head at the diner. "My father and I put a new roof on that building when I was fourteen."

"Yes, sir. The new owners, though . . ." The officer left the sentence unfinished.

Owen held back the temptation to mention the peeling paint and the askew screen door on the diner. The place felt abandoned and neglected by whoever owned it now. These weren't matters that would interest the Mountie, and there was more pressing business to deal with. "I got in late last night and couldn't think of anywhere else to go," Owen said. "I always stayed with my parents—" He stopped, realizing the officer wouldn't care about his family history, either. "I didn't damage anything." He shifted a few centimetres to the left, trying to block the officer's view of the hasp dangling behind him. "I was going to sleep under those trees by the lake, but it was too cold. I didn't think anyone would mind," he added.

"We come down here fairly regularly. Teenagers like to party on the beach. Build campfires. We keep an eye on things so they don't get out of hand," the officer said.

"I partied down here a few times myself," Owen replied. "Many years ago."

"I'm going to have to ask you to come with me, sir. Until we get this cleared up. I'll have to speak with the owners." He paused. "If you'll just put on a shirt and some shoes, we can be on our way."

"What about my things? The car?"

"We'll take care of those later," the officer said. "Once we get everything sorted out."

Owen went back inside and got dressed. When he emerged from the cabin, the officer indicated the trunk of the police cruiser. "Please empty your pockets and put everything there."

Owen pulled out his wallet, passport, cell phone, car keys and a fistful of coins. The officer gave him a quick but thorough pat-down before pulling a card from his breast pocket. Owen was used to hearing the Miranda warning on American TV. It had been a while, though, since he'd heard the Charter Caution.

"Do you understand your rights?"

Owen nodded.

The officer placed Owen's belongings in a plastic bag after pocketing his passport. "If I don't put you in handcuffs, you won't cause me any trouble, will you, sir?"

"I'll behave," Owen said. He sat quietly in the back seat as the officer drove up the gravel road and rejoined the road to Chipman, which was now part of the village of Grand Lake. On the way, they drove by the house where Owen had grown up, which his parents had built, buying lumber and other supplies as they could afford them. He remembered the crunching sound car tires made on the gravel driveway. As they passed, Owen saw that the new occupants had fenced off part of the backyard. Horses now grazed where his parents once kept a vegetable garden.

After his mother died, he'd spent a week sorting through the house's contents, trying to decide what to keep, what to donate, and what to throw into the dumpster he'd rented. The "to keep" pile hadn't been very big, when all was said and done. Afterward, he'd sold the place without ever meeting the people who'd bought it. Giving up the house that had been part of his life for over forty years hurt more than he cared to admit, but keeping it wasn't feasible. It still didn't seem right that strangers lived there now.

A kilometre farther up the road, they passed what used to be a United Church. As a kid, he had helped his father finish the basement, paint the steeple, and install a stained-glass window in the choir loft. It wasn't a church anymore, though. After more than a century of services, baptisms, confirmations, weddings, and funerals, the pastoral charge had decommissioned the building when the shrinking congregation could no longer support it. The last he'd heard, it had become a carpenter's workshop. Jesus might approve, Owen thought.

The cemetery where his parents were buried was across the road. His mother had always been a frequent visitor to the graveyard, but Owen had no desire to see his parents' names etched in marble. This tiny community, little more than a populated stretch of rural highway, had once been Owen's anchor to the world. His wife, who had never spent more than three years in any one house before they married, hadn't understood why he continued to call it "back home." To her, home was where they currently lived, not a place from the past.

He should have visited more often, he chided himself. He hadn't realized how much he would miss the place. On the other hand, given how things had turned out on this trip so far, maybe he should have stayed away.

The road into Chipman took them past other familiar landmarks: the bridge where a hitchhiker had taught him to fish with a worm and a safety pin; the tiny house where his father had grown up with a dozen siblings. Once, Owen could have named every person in every house along the way. In later years, Sunday afternoon phone calls with his parents—a ritual he missed as much as he missed them—had kept him up to date about who had fallen, who had suffered a heart attack, and who had died. Funerals had become a regular addition to their social calendar.

The RCMP detachment was located behind Chipman Forest Avenue School, which Owen had attended for grades six through twelve. The Mountie led Owen inside and told him to wait on a hard plastic chair next to a cluttered desk after offering him a cup of coffee, which Owen accepted. The solitary holding cell at the back of the room was currently empty. Owen wondered if that was where he would be spending the night. It couldn't be any less comfortable than the wooden bunk he'd slept on the night before, he told himself.

While he waited to learn his fate, a man in a brown uniform carrying several packages stopped at the desk. The man, who appeared to be about Owen's age, peered at him. "I know you, don't I?" he asked. "Owen, right? We graduated together."

Owen searched his memory. His graduating class hadn't been all that big, but his memory for names had never been good.

"I'm Dave. Dave Steward. What are you doing here?"

"A little misunderstanding that I hope will get straightened out before long."

"You went to Dal, didn't you? Became a scientist or something like that?"

Owen admitted that, yes, he indeed had become a scientist.

"Where are you living now?"

"In Texas," Owen said, although he wasn't sure that was true anymore.

"I thought you went overseas."

"For a couple of years, yeah. Postdoc."

Steward frowned as if the term was unfamiliar but he didn't ask, so Owen didn't feel the need to explain.

"Haven't seen you in ages."

Owen shrugged. "I don't get back much."

"I usually stop by the lounge at the inn for a few beers when I get off work. It'd be great to catch up."

"I might be a little tied up," Owen said, holding up his hands as if he were in cuffs.

"Sure," Steward said with a forced laugh. "Anyhow, I have to take care of these," he said, hefting the packages.

Owen nodded and the man went on his way.

Fifteen minutes later, the Mountie returned. "Okay, Mr. Cook. Good news. I spoke to the campground owner and he's decided not to press charges. You're free to go."

Owen got to his feet and thanked the officer. He half expected to be warned to get out of town by sundown, but that didn't happen. "What about my car and stuff?" he asked.

"Everything's out in the parking lot."

"Okay, thanks again. Sorry for the trouble."

"Have a nice day, Mr. Cook." He escorted Owen to the front desk to retrieve his personal effects.

When he got to his rental, Owen found the urn containing his wife's ashes sitting on the passenger seat, held in place by the seatbelt. He wondered what the officer who had searched his luggage thought about that.

He hadn't yet decided yet what to do with Lucy's ashes. Her parents, who were getting on in years, said they didn't want them. He thought about spreading them in the Gulf of Mexico, but the water there was so polluted it seemed like an insult. He'd almost scattered them in the lake the night before, but that hadn't seemed right, either. Inspiration would surely strike at some point. All he knew was that he wasn't taking them back to Texas.

The Queen's County Inn was the only place in town he knew to get breakfast, so he drove down Main Street, took the bridge across Salmon River and pulled into the inn's parking lot, which was across the street from his old elementary school.

His server looked vaguely familiar. Her nametag identified her as Carrie, and after a few seconds of reflection he realized she was Carla's younger sister. That brought back a flood of warm memories. She gave him a knowing smile that was very much like his high-school girlfriend's. "I thought I recognized you," she said. "What are you doing back in town?"

"Just passing through," Owen said.

"Have you seen Carla? She'd get a kick out of knowing you were around. She talks about you every now and then."

Owen wasn't sure how to respond to that. "How is she?"

"Keeping busy with the twins," Carrie said. "Are you staying at the inn?"

Her resemblance to her sister was striking, and he found himself wondering what Carla looked like now. Married with kids, apparently. They had been an item all through high school and had even tried to make the long-distance thing work when he went to university. That had only lasted a few months. Not a painful breakup, for him at least, but a breakup nonetheless, his first. He'd seen her in passing a few times over the years, but they'd never really spoken again.

He emerged from his reverie, realizing he'd been staring at Carrie for too long without answering. "No. Like I said, just passing through."

Only two other tables were occupied in the restaurant, so Carrie frequently stopped to check on him and refill his coffee mug. "You ended up somewhere down south, didn't you?" she asked on one of her visits. "New Orleans?"

"Houston," he said.

"Big change from Chipman, I'll bet," she said.

He nodded. He'd never intended to stay in Texas. The job there had been a stepping stone after his postdoctoral position in Switzerland. However, he'd done well with the company and then he'd met the woman who would become his wife at a party thrown by mutual friends. Lucy became his new anchor, rooting him in Houston. He remembered an oft-repeated line from a romantic comedy they'd enjoyed: "If you love someone, that's where you belong."

So, Owen had belonged in Houston—until his wife died. Now he no longer knew where he belonged. Without Lucy and the lifelong bedrock of his hometown, Owen felt adrift, like an astronaut whose mooring line had been severed. They had assumed they'd be together for a lifetime, never realizing how poorly defined that word could be.

He'd taken a temporary leave of absence from his job after she died. While contemplating this trip, he'd considered making it permanent. He thought he might buy a house up here, somewhere near the lake, and write a novel. The exchange rate was very much in his favour if he sold the place in Texas. Lucy had always encouraged him to write, but he'd never found the time. Now, he couldn't imagine what he'd been thinking. The nostalgia he felt was for a place that was long gone. Thomas Wolfe had been right.

He left a nice tip for Carrie and smiled at her on the way out of the restaurant. After he made one more loop around the village, he pulled into the Shoppers Drug Mart parking lot while he gathered his thoughts. The Lotto 6/49 sign in the window seemed like a come-on, tempting him to roll the dice to help decide whether to stay or go.

He could be in Halifax in less than four hours, roughly the same amount of time it would take him to get back to Bangor. He'd spent most of his twenties in Halifax and had many fond memories of the city. Or he could head north and across to Quebec City and points beyond. That was the thing about being adrift—he could go wherever he wanted.

But what did he want?

He couldn't leave without one last visit to the lake, though. He found a vantage point where he could—without trespassing—look across to the far side and the campground where he'd been arrested a few hours ago. He could almost hear a fiddle and a piano, the music of his childhood; could almost smell the smoke from a bonfire, the aroma of buttered corn and steamed clams; could almost hear laughter and jovial conversation; could almost taste the sugary raspberry Kool-Aid the kids drank until they were bouncing off the walls, and the beer that came later. It was all a dream, though. A vision of the past.

He got back in the car and continued south, barely glancing at the house where he grew up as he went by. That wasn't home any longer. When he reached the intersection with the highway, he pulled onto the shoulder of the road. The sensation of being adrift made him think about tides, which in turn called to mind the Bay of Fundy, which had the highest tides in the world. The bay seemed a better choice than Grand Lake, which was too confined.

He could be in Point Wolfe in an hour and a half. From there he could take a trail to the bay. He'd once promised Lucy, an avid outdoor enthusiast, that he would take her hiking along parts of the Trans Canada Trail, but they never managed to find the time when visiting his parents. Now he would finally make good on that vow.

He stopped for some granola bars and bottled water at the Fundy General Store in Alma, along with a small backpack to put everything in, then paid for his entry permit to Fundy National Park at the Headquarters Visitor Center.

It wasn't yet noon when he crossed the famous covered red bridge. He parked well away from the only other car in the lot at the trailhead and packed his backpack with his provisions and the sealed plastic bag from inside the urn containing Lucy's ashes.

Although there were shorter routes, he picked the Goose River Trail, which would take about two-and-a-half hours in each direction, according to a sign at the entrance. Allowing for some time at the beach at the far end, he could finish the round trip before it got too dark. He slung the pack over his back and set out.

The salt-tinged air smelled of rich loam and decaying leaves, and on top of the sound of his feet crunching on the gravel path he could hear running water and the call of birds. Among the deadfalls and downed limbs scattered beneath the spruce, fir, maple and birch trees, he found a strong branch long enough to use as a walking stick, which helped when the trail ascended and descended. Wearing sneakers probably wasn't the best decision, he thought after he almost lost his footing for the second time, but it was cool enough that there were no mosquitoes or black flies, at least.

Instead of waiting to reach Goose River Beach, Owen started distributing his wife's ashes along the way. A squirrel nattered at him when he scattered a handful from a wooden bridge that spanned a burbling brook and another amongst a patch of mossy earth to one side of the trail. It made it seem more like Lucy was on the hike with him.

Every now and then, the trees opened up to his left to yield panoramic views of the Bay of Fundy. The sky was deep blue, adorned with wispy cirrus clouds. He could see across the bay to the far side, which might have been the Nova Scotia coastline. He wasn't sure.

Although the trail was well maintained, he had to clamber over fallen trees in a couple of places, and step gingerly through a section where a brook overran the path. He paused to collect his breath after some of the steeper ascents, and his legs were going to make him pay for this trek tomorrow, but he finally reached the point where the trail led down to the beach. This was the steepest descent of his journey, made all the more challenging by the strong breeze coming in from the coast. Fortunately, there were wooden steps part of the way down.

Pine trees lined the bluffs on both sides of the valley like vigilant sentinels. The tide was receding, leaving behind wide, flat patches on the beach. Jagged, weather-worn rocks jutted from tidal pools. Owen found a starfish in one, which seemed like a good omen. There were a couple of camping spots with fire pits and low stone walls for protection against the marine breeze, but he was alone today on this isolated beach.

He approached the shoreline and stared out at the placid bay, whose waters, like those of the Gulf of Mexico, connected to the Atlantic and beyond. As he sprinkled the last of Lucy's ashes into the water to be carried away by the ebbing tide, he imagined some of her residual molecules storming up the Petitcodiac River as part of the Tidal Bore or flowing into the Saint John River and up the Reversing Falls. They might drift all the way to Europe or Africa. Or back to Texas, even. Given enough time, parts of her could be everywhere.

When he got back to the car, exhausted but exhilarated, he wondered which way the tides would carry him. He still had the return portion of his airline ticket and a house in Houston filled with the

ADRIFT

things he and Lucy accumulated over a dozen years. Did he still belong there? Was that home?

He'd soon have to decide. He headed north to pick up the highway again. From there, the road, like the ocean, went on forever.

It was dark when he reached the interchange and turned onto the highway. He set the cruise control, found a classic rock station on the radio and continued driving into the night.

Roadside Reunion

BILL ENGLESON

British Columbia | Kettle Valley Rail–McCulloch to Midway

Ricky was more excited than he thought he'd be. It had been over twelve months since he had seen his mother. It wasn't that he actually *wanted* to see her. He was still pissed at her.

She had been less than helpful when he had been arrested for beating and kicking and ripping off the stupid old bitch who had been asking for it, like she didn't know that if you walked around that neighbourhood at night with a big fat purse, someone was going to make a grab for it.

When the cops came to the door, when they had literally busted down the door because they knew he was in there and his old lady was passed out totally blotto on the couch, and he certainly wasn't of a mind to let the cops in, well, they broke in anyways and found him hiding in his bedroom closet. They'd hauled him away in cuffs and called an ambulance for his old drunk mother.

Any decent parent would have sobered up, would have defended their child in court, would have done whatever was necessary to protect their baby. Not his mother. She had come to the hearing stoned out of her mind, all loud and useless. That's when his legal aid lawyer had said, "Kid, you are screwed. Not just screwed. Screwed, blued, and tattooed. No court in the land is going to send you home to that. You're going away, bucko. And quickly if I'm any judge. It'll do you good, believe you me. You know what they say, what doesn't kill ya . . ." For some reason, his lawyer decided not to finish what he was saying. What an asshole he was, thought Ricky. Of course, the asshole *wasn't* a judge. He wasn't even much of a lawyer. He didn't care what was going on with Ricky. Hell, he probably even got a bonus for getting his client to plead guilty and save all that court time.

When he was sentenced a few weeks later, grudgingly agreeing to attend the Hope Springs Eternal Mountain Youth Camp, his old lady had shown up for the sentencing more sober than she'd been in years. She'd even blubbered and thrown her arms around him so the judge could see that she was a loving mother, even if she was a bit of a souse, and, more than just a loving mother, she'd stood by her little boy in his hour of need.

It had, unfortunately, turned out to be much longer than one hour of need. It had been hundreds and thousands of hours, many months that he had been stuffed away in the woods, surrounded by horseshit, human toads, and a few religious nuts who just wouldn't let up about work, God, and manure. *His* hour of need would *never* end at the rate it was going.

That was pretty much why he was excited about the prospect of his mother getting driven up to Rock Creek. It would give him a shot at getting in touch with his old, pre-Hope Springs life. He had a great need to have something from *before*. Something to remind him of the past, to remind him that the past was still there to get back to, that the past was not a lost cause. He wanted to get back to the way it once was, even if that meant seeing his screw-up of a mother. He needed to get away from the dust, the smelly cowboys, and all the fucking animals of the youth prison. He was kind of desperate, he had to admit.

He finally got up out of his bunk. The breakfast gong had clanged ten minutes earlier. His three roomies were squirming around taking as much time as they could squeeze to stay in bed. They'd all had a

NOT THE SAME ROAD OUT

few compulsory chores to do before breakfast. Shovelling shit. It was enough to turn your stomach. Manure, please. Shovelling manure. You could call horseshit or cow shit peppermint if you wanted but it would still smell like shit to Ricky. Like manure, he corrected himself.

The noxious smells of the country had been clinging to his nose from the day he arrived. Every second of every minute.

His probation officer, John Polson, had driven him up to Rock Creek, special. Just the two of them on a nine-hour drive. Before coming to the camp, he couldn't remember another time where he had spent so much time in one sitting with one adult. Maybe with his mom, but they had never had that easy way of being together, a comfortable give and take sort of relationship. Maybe when he was younger, but he doubted it. She was always wound up, except when she was drunk, when she became a zombie.

He'd had a few child care workers over the years with whom he'd spent small chunks of time, but it was usually an hour here and a bowling game there. But the trip upcountry to the Hopeless Sprung a Leak Camp had been something different. Polson hadn't talked all that much but occasionally he'd tried to extract some commentary from Ricky. Like when he had pretty much repeated his spiel about how great the camp was.

"You may not be showing it, Ricky, but you've got to be excited about this experience. It's one heck of an opportunity."

There they were, on the road, heading for some godforsaken prison camp and John Polson had the balls to suggest this whole charade was an "opportunity." It was rah-rah crap like this that reinforced Ricky's lack of respect for adults. Instead of just leaving it alone, or calling it what it was, they had to put a stupidly happy spin on it.

He'd looked at Polson and smiled. He was tempted to say

something sharp and snarky but was beginning to wise up some. While he couldn't fathom what the opportunity was, and no amount of adult blah blah would ever make it fathomable, he did understand that the alternative to attending the camp was incarceration at juvie. Neither seemed a good choice but a choice had to be made, and he had gone with the friggin' wilderness.

"I've had a couple of boys go up to Hope Springs before, Ricky," John Polson had stated as they were close to the drop off point. "It wasn't a miracle cure for them by any means, no magical solution, but they both later thanked me for the opportunity. In the beginning, neither of them was chomping at the bit to go. Both were hard-core city kids. One had never even ridden a horse before—just like you."

Ricky wanted to lash back and say that he had never wanted to ride a stupid horse, but he knew, and John Polson likely knew, that that was a crock. Every kid he had ever known wanted to ride a horse. And he *had* ridden a horse. Almost. Once. Keith, one of his many childcare workers, had promised to take him one Saturday. There was a small riding centre at the bottom of Cariboo Road. Keith said he'd taken several kids he'd worked with in the past riding there. Ricky had been all primed except Keith had called the night before and said that he had to make a quick trip out of town to be with his sister who'd been injured in a car accident. His sister had kids and needed him to help her and that was that. Ricky never saw him again.

It was a couple of months before they assigned a new childcare worker. That one had been a bust. Pathetic loser had fallen off horses a couple of times growing up and had absolutely no interest in trying that again. That dick was so courageous that he had taken up bowling. "No one ever broke their neck bowling," what's-his-face had said.

"I'm not taking you all the way in, Rick. I've been there once before. It's a gruelling trip off the highway. Need a four-wheeler to make it doable. The important part is making sure the staff know you and you meet them. At least, one of them. Whoever they send."

That felt *so* good, knowing that John Polson would hand him off to whatever cowfucker happened to show up. Like he was a piece of meat, or, maybe one of those fucking relay batons. The kind that sometimes got dropped and kicked to the ground. He'd almost made the relay team in Grade 7. Would have to if he'd gone to school on a regular basis. He liked running. Hard running. It was one of the few useful things school had taught him. He knew most anybody could run, but he'd learned about breathing, accelerating, the beauty of speed. He loved running because you could always just up and get away. At least in the city. Most of the time. Except the last time. And that didn't count for the cops. They got him cold at home. Being a good runner couldn't have helped there—or here.

"I don't want to go, John. I'll die there. I know I will."

John Polson, who had some blubber on him and was clearly suffering from the wretchedly hot weather, put a smile on his chubby face and said, "I seriously doubt that you'll die, Ricky. Look over there." He nodded to his left. "You see those people on bikes? They're riding on an old railbed, goes all the way to Hope, just to enjoy the outdoors. For *fun*."

Ricky wasn't going to bother responding to that. Fifteen minutes later, John Polson told him they were close to the rendezvous spot.

"Right," he had replied.

Then he had slipped into his shell. He reasoned, as best as he could, that if you are a worthless package being handed off to some wilderness mountain man, you might as well stay all wrapped up. The rendezvous-point was pretty much a chunk of dirt, an unpaved road, not much more than a goat path that had been squeezed out of the mountains like a pimple that intersected with the main highway.

ROADSIDE REUNION

John Polson had pulled over against a high bank. A dried-up skinny tree, its roots exposed in the slope of the bank, a few of its gnarly tentacles sticking out of the dusty soil, provided a skeleton of shade for them. As they waited, Ricky fell into more of a funk. Most of his life, he had been able to see a way out, some possible escape. Here, scrunched up against the earthen bank, trapped in the car with law-and-order Polson, waiting to be dragged into the mountains for an unspecified time, he tried one more pitch for freedom.

He then added, "You'll hate it at first. They'll work you hard. It's part ranch, part sawmill. You'll learn to carry your weight. You've never had to do that before. If there was ever a chance of you becoming a whole man, this is it."

Ricky was steaming mad, both from the heat and the lecture. He had heard the same words before from someone, maybe Polson or his lawyer. They all sounded the same to him: voices that had nothing new to offer.

They both heard the sound of a vehicle approaching. It was there before they could catch their breath. It was a big old beat-up pickup truck with a hoist on the back. The driver spun a soft slow u-ey on the empty highway and pulled up beside John Polson's car. The driver reached over to his passenger door, opened it, and slid over to exit. He looked burnt—a short man with a brown face covered by a wide-brimmed stained cowboy hat. His boots were huge. He slipped out of the truck and walked the two feet to John Polson's open driver's window. He then stuck out his hand and John Polson reciprocated. "Sam Butterworth. You Polson?"

"I certainly am, Mr. Butterworth. This is Ricky Doucette," he added, pointing somewhat uselessly in Ricky's direction.

"I figured," replied Butterworth. "Hey, son," he offered. No handshake. Just, "hey, son."

"Okay," said John Polson, maybe picking up on the strain all around as he got out of the car. "Grab your bag, Ricky."

NOT THE SAME ROAD OUT

"Rick," Ricky said, too loudly, "I want to be called Rick."

"Rick it is," said Butterworth, stepping away from the car door to allow John Polson space. "Throw your gear in the back of the truck, Rick."

The transfer was over quickly. Polson gave Sam an envelope and said, "He was medicalled at the detention centre so he's as healthy as a horse. A little soft maybe, but nothing is out of whack. Could you give this envelope to your boss? It's got whatever we know about young Ricky in it."

"Hmmm, don't think of Pastor Barnes as my boss," Sam Butterworth said. "He's the paper-pusher guy. I'll pass it along next time he comes to camp." Ricky looked at Polson to see what he thought of Butterworth's declaration about his "boss." Polson didn't seem to pick up what seemed obvious to Ricky. Sam Butterworth didn't take orders from anyone.

Butterworth got back in the cab of the pick-up the same way he had exited, via the passenger door. "Got to get the driver's door fixed soon. Hop in, Rick. See ya, Polson."

With that concise exchange completed, the drive into the dusty Midway Range began.

For the first fifteen minutes or so, they were both quiet. The initial part of the road was a slow go. Sam Butterworth was paying close attention to every twist and turn. Then the road, if that's what it was, became a bumpy rollercoaster of pot-holed torture.

"It gets better later, Rick lad. This first bit might shake you up a bit. It gets most everybody, even me."

As they climbed up the hilly countryside, and then, occasionally, dipped into a gully, only to scramble up and out again, Rick began to pay more attention to the road they were on. Roads, really, because there seemed to be a bunch of them. It soon became evident to him that this rocky landscape was littered with a tangled mess of branches, paths, and endless trails that crept off into the underbrush, disappearing as if by magic, some dark evil magic. Keeping track of any of them was next to pointless.

As if he was reading Ricky's mind, Sam Butterworth made a frighteningly accurate comment. "You look like you're paying close attention to every twist and turn, Rick. That's good. It's wise to know where you've been and where you are going to end up. Trouble is, I doubt it's gonna help you backtrack, if that's what you're thinking. Is it?"

That was exactly what he *was* pondering. It was what anyone would do. But Sam Butterworth was right. There were so many curves in the road, twists and turns galore. He could stare at the road and try to remember the way they were going, the way back, but it was a spider's web of confusion, and he had lost his way a while before.

"Before I joined up with Harry Barnes and the Hope Springs Eternal Ministry—they run the camp in case you didn't know—the story was that they had this particular kid who was ordered by the court to stay at the camp. Like you, some kids get ordered here by the law. Some, well they just wear their folks out and get dropped off. Anyway, whatever his real name was, everyone, I've been told, called this little tumbleweed Zippo. Zippo was always sneaking off for a smoke, clutching his daddy's lighter like a lifeline. Thing is, in the summer especially, these mountains are a tinderbox. Apparently, Zippo didn't much care about that. He was one of those little freaks, you've probably met a few like him, it's all about them, right? They don't give two hoots about anyone else, about fire in the hills, about nothing except whatever it is they want. Well, I'm told Zippo got so upset the last time his ciggie was snatched out of his mouth that he just up and took off. Now, when someone runs off into these hills, especially at night, no one in their right mind is going to go looking for them. It would be just plain suicide. We don't have the manpower to do a night search. So, the truth is no one went looking for Zippo. Maybe he made it out. But he never went home again and, as far as I know, he was a goner. His bones have likely been picked clean by vultures and are stacked in a little pile on some lonely hillside. Maybe up there," and Sam Butterworth pointed the finger of his right hand off in the distance to a faraway hill. His hand then dropped down and touched Rick's left knee, almost like it was an accident. He then placed that same hand on the steering wheel. And then Sam Butterworth shut up. He had made his point. Rick didn't know if he believed the hogwash he'd just heard but he did know that it was probably easy to get lost up here. You didn't have to be Davy friggin' Crockett to figure that out.

Ricky Doucette had almost lost track of time. Sometimes it seemed to him that he was doomed never to leave this camp, this horseshit reformatory, this hellish there-ain't-no-fucking-hope fucked up mountain prison camp. An entire year had worn away. One earlier planned visit with his mother had been ditched. Heavy snowfall, they said. He'd complained, "You're keeping me a prisoner!" Nobody disagreed. "Well, there is some truth to that, little Ricky," Sam Butterworth droned on at his assholier-than-thou, put-downer best. "This is a correctional facility, bucko. And if anyone ever needed correcting, it's you."

"Go gentle on the lad, Sam," Pastor Barnes, the nominal, often absent, head cheese of the camp had advised that day. Harry Barnes and his Hope Springs Eternal Ministry were in charge, but the minister only came once a week at best and frequently less. And the cheerful preacher didn't know dick about the place. That was clear to Ricky.

Today, Barnes shook his hand. "Have a good visit, Rick. You're not the tough nut you were when you arrived. We're hoping we can point you out as a real success story."

Bullishly, Sam Butterworth added, "Yup, you haven't mugged any old ladies in a year. We must be doing something right."

ROADSIE REUNION

"Sam!" Barnes raised his voice.

"Sorry, Harry. Keep forgetting you're here."

"You'd do well to remember who's in charge, Sam. And what we are trying to achieve with these young men."

"We'd better get going. It's a long drive to the meet-up point."

With Sam's slippery sidestep from an uncomfortable reprimand done with, he and Ricky got in the camp's new Jeep and headed out. For the first bit of rough road, they were both clam-silent. Sam was steaming. Ricky had seen that side of the head wrangler several times. He knew to keep a lid on it until Sam gave permission to speak. He stared out the window, watching steep valleys appear and disappear as they wound their way down the mountain through stands of ponderosa pine.

He thought about what he wanted to say his mother. Mostly it was, "Get me the hell outta Manureville." There were so many secrets locked down in these mountains. No one cared—no one wanted to hear. He had to admit one truth about the place, though, about his time in the mountains: he had learned some shit. Mostly that he liked getting physically stronger. They had worked the bejesus out of him. Clearing trails, hauling out flammable underbrush, fishing, cooking, things he had never done before. There had also been the early morning runs. Running had once been his thing. The runs had progressed from a few hundred yards to the point where he could once again run five miles at a clip. Also that winter, the mini marathons were frequently topped off by mandatory jumping into a freezing mountain stream.

All of this he knew would serve him well on the streets of the Lower Mainland.

Sam finally busted the tense stillness and Ricky's brief reverie. "We'll just about make your damned appointment, little Ricky. All this trouble for a one-hour visit with your old lady and whoever drove her drunken ass up."

Sam then reached over and gripped Ricky's thigh hard.

"You haven't fooled me none, sweet cheeks. A month, maybe two, you'll be back in the city. Nobody checking up on you, running your own ragged little life! You'll be so fucking tempted. Squirming and sweating in your bed in whatever hovel you and your crazy old lady live in. Then, one delicious night, it'll all burst outta you. Like puss from a popped boil. That's when you're going to creep for sure. You'll be creepy crawling outta your hole, stalking old ladies, beaning, and bagging them. Maybe kill some!"

Ricky sat frozen. He hated Sam Butterworth for a bucket of reasons. He hated him most because it was like Sam had deep drilled into his brain, stolen his most private, most scary thoughts, knew his every fear.

"You're nothing but a train wreck in the making, buddy boy."

Even if it was a new Jeep, Ricky's butt was in agony. He almost wept to see the highway. God he missed pavement. He spotted the G-car. They all looked the same: plain and simple—usually dirty. Sometimes with an insignia. Often not. Sometimes it was their personal wheels. Cheap cars to blend in, but once they got out of their cars, they stood out like what they were: trouble.

He watched his old lady scramble out of the passenger side and rush over to his side of the Jeep. Ricky got out, stretched, and she grabbed him like he was a life-preserver, not a deep bearhug, more like a hug that frail old fucks might give each other. She released him, stepped back, said, "You look good."

He didn't *feel* good, but he knew what she meant. The year of slave labour had done wonders for his physique. He knew that and was pleased about that part. Never really big, he had grown at least an inch and was now five foot eight. He heard Sam get out while his mother was mauling him.

Ricky glanced back at the G-car as the goober who'd drove his mother up headed over to Sam and said, "Wally Rose, support worker."

Sam replied, in his grainy, shitty voice, "Sam Butterworth, lead hand at Hope Springs Eternal. I expected Gerry, too?"

"Yeah," Rose said, "I called him from the gas station down the road. He can't make it."

"No big loss. Visit's an hour. Then I have to head back."

"Yeah," Rose answered. "That was my understanding. An hour, give or take."

"No," Sam laid down Sam's law. "An hour, tops. These kids are doing time. We don't give it away."

The ground rules were set. Clearly there was no negotiation. No slack available. He and his mother found a patch of flat earth and sat down and began to eat the lunch Social Services had packed for them. The Rose guy offered Butterworth a couple of cheese sandwiches, but he declined. "Nah, I'm good. I'll just join little Ricky and his dear old mom and listen in."

"Perhaps we should give them some privacy," Ricky heard Rose suggest.

"Nope, not in the cards. He's in our care. No privacy for these big bad boys."

With that, Butterworth ambled over to where they were seated and planted himself next to Ricky like a leech. Then Rose hustled over and plunked himself down as well. It didn't raise the temperature, but it didn't seem right.

He and his mom went silent for a bit. Just sitting there thinking, not thinking. Just sitting in the sun. She looked okay, no worse than the last time he saw her, and seemed sober. She'd spent nine hours in a car with Wally fucking Rose, just to sit here for an hour. Ricky had to admit that wasn't nothing.

Fifteen minutes later, Rose asked Butterworth, "How much time do we have before you head out?" Sam looked at his wristwatch, said, "Half an hour. Wish I could stretch it, but we bend the rules, these slippery little buggers will squeeze as much juice out of us as they can."

Ricky looked at the Rose guy who wasn't hiding his view that Sam was a piece of work. With no local PO at the visit, Sam was making out that he was the boss. Rose didn't seem to want to jockey for that position. What a pussy.

"Let us know when we're over the limit." Rose said to Sam. Then, "Rick, I'll leave you and your mom alone to spend some good time together, but I wanted to introduce myself and mention that my job will be to assist the two of you to live together successfully once you are released."

It was a mouthful of information and news to Ricky. Before Rose wandered off to plunk his butt on a rock, he said, "Your mom can tell you. You and I will chat, if you are willing, just before you head back."

His mom nodded, said, "Thanks, Mr. Rose."

Ricky watched Rose take up a position on a large rock and start to soak up a few rays. An easy job, Ricky thought. Just hanging out on a sunny day. His mother put on a sober smile and seemed to be savouring the brief time Butterworth's fixed, arbitrary backwoods rules were allowing her. Ricky hated being under anyone's thumb. His mother yakked away, and he zoned out.

In a month or so, he'd get sprung. He'd then be transported back to live with her. Probably by this Rose guy, or a PO. Or even Sam Butterworth.

Then they'd be in the thick of it. A permanent fucking tearful mother–son reunion. Until it wasn't. He couldn't imagine it playing out well. Spinning wheels. That's what it would be like. Spinning wheels and wasting everyone's time.

He could hardly wait.

So Late in the Season

TRICIA SNELL

Nova Scotia | Rum Runners Trail

"True North," Edward tells Rachel, because she mentioned a possibility of getting some web design work from True North Media, "is actually the term for the geographic North Pole, where lines of longitude converge on maps." It's also a right-wing media fiasco that doesn't care about the truth, he wants to say, but doesn't. He's not sure she knows that.

"Oh, interesting," Rachel says.

He's already told her he is a real estate agent and a historian. He studied history at university. He won't mention his orienteering passion. But he can't help but add, "Magnetic North, on the other hand, is where the needle points on an old-fashioned compass. It aligns with the Earth's magnetic field, which points directly downwards through the exact centre of the planet."

"Hmmm," she says, slipping her hand under her long hair and using her fingers to comb it out.

"Migrating animals—sea turtles, for instance, and certain birds and fish like salmon—use the Magnetic North to navigate their routes." Edward thinks it's remarkable that humans don't seem to naturally sense the Magnetic North, the way animals do.

But he sees her eyes—are they green? That's rare—losing focus, so he instead says, "You have beautiful hair."

She smiles. "Thank you. When the salons closed, that was it for me." Her hair is salt and pepper at the top, ash brown at the wavy ends. "I know it's different from the photo I posted on Elite Singles."

Until Covid, he hadn't known how many women had white or grey hair. He thinks the way women stride along the street now, their silver hair flying, feels fresh and icy, no longer dulled by Hot Toffee or Midnight Ruby dye.

"Even though they're open again," Rachel continues, "all those chemicals, no, I won't. Plus, the time, the money, it's too much of a pain in the ass." She pronounces it *ahhhss*. Her profile says she's from South Africa, and that she is somewhere between thirty-five and fifty. He himself is fifty-five. "Salons have a name for my hair now—a 'reverse ombré.' That's putting a bright spin on it. They don't say 'your roots are showing' anymore!"

Edward smiles. "It looks great," he says. He would have said "beautiful," but he doesn't want to come on too strong. Her eyes are in fact a dazzling green when they catch the light. Funny, though, he isn't feeling much chemistry. Not like the chemistry he once had with Lisa.

The barista finally calls out their order, and he gets up to fetch their drinks.

Edward chose this place on Montague Street, the coolest coffee shop in Lunenburg, or in the whole of the South Shore of Nova Scotia, in his opinion, because he thought it would be reasonably quiet, good for conversation. Who knew that on a Thursday afternoon in October, with tourist season over, the place would be buzzing? Full of people avoiding the rain, he supposes.

He weaves in and out of the packed tables and the people standing in the aisles chatting. It feels more like a bar than a coffee shop. The window overlooking the street is fogged up from the rain that's persisted since morning, and the air is frigid. Snow can't come this early, he thinks, but it feels as if fall is aiming hard toward winter.

The barista has set Edward's and Rachel's drinks on the edge of the counter. She has short hair, a sweet Peter-Pan cap that's a mix of grey-mauve and blond, as if the sun and moon worked together to create this blend. There's a touch of Japanese anime about her, Edward thinks, her eyes all eyeliner and shadow in the same mauve as her hair. Silver hoops and sparkling studs up the sides of her ears. Her hands seem to sparkle too, sleek with sink water, sinewy, and now pointing with her mauve (once again) polished nails at Rachel's latté and his Americano.

Walking back to Rachel at their table, he sees she is gazing out at the rainy street, lost in thought. He has a sudden, desperate stab of loneliness. He guesses she is not thinking about him. What is he doing here on this date with her?

When he puts her latté on the table before him, she smiles and lifts it to blow on its frothy surface, but she does not say thank you.

Well, nothing to do but to get through the coffee with her and then let it all gently drift away. He's had a few awkward dates lately. He should take the Elite Singles app off his phone. And the eHarmony one.

Settled across from her again, he asks, "Do you enjoy living on Heckman's Island?" Besides the fact that she's a web designer, it's the only thing he knows about her for sure.

"I do." She takes a sip, then puts her cup down quickly. "Just a minute, do you mind?" She points to her black leather bag, sitting at her feet. A phone is vibrating from somewhere in its interior.

"Oh, yes, go ahead!" He does find it rude, but he wouldn't say so.

"I wouldn't normally, but . . . My son, he's just eleven and . . ." She pushes her chair back, answers her phone, extracts a paisley-patterned facemask from her pocket, and removes one of her sculpted silver earrings all at once. He recognizes the earring design from a jeweller on Lincoln Street; he's the agent who sold that building to its current owner.

NOT THE SAME ROAD OUT

He sips his Americano and watches Rachel navigate through all the coffee drinkers to the door. Eleven. An eleven-year-old is a lot to contend with. His kids—James, twenty, now in university, and Fiona, seventeen, in Grade 12—they live with Lisa in Halifax, about an hour up the coast by car. Covid was a huge interruption to both of them, and to him. Edward missed the last three Christmases with them, since Lisa did not include him in their Covid-19 "social pod."

In his first communication with Rachel before this date, he painted his relationship with James and Fiona in glowing terms. But the truth is, they grew up during the Covid years in ways that feel alien to him. At worst, he fears he is losing them, though in more confident moments, he thinks they probably still love him.

He will be seeing Fiona tomorrow. He hopes it goes well.

Through the foggy, rain-streaked window, he can see the distorted shape of Rachel on the sidewalk, close to the building, head down, phone pressed to her ear. She must be freezing, though she looks capable and comfortable in her burgundy sweater, dark skirt, and flat-soled ankle boots. A lot like Lisa, in fact. Why is he not more attracted to Rachel? She appears to be confident, independent, honest, even funny (that comment about reverse ombré was funny, and honest). Same as Lisa.

Her web designer career is about on par with his real estate agent one, neither remarkable nor completely boring.

He shifts in his seat. He worries that Rachel's latté will get cold, and he'd like to be home. It's only four, but the rain is turning into a storm, and the sky is dark, almost like evening all of a sudden. He tugs at the collar of his shirt. It cuts into his neck in an irritating way. It's a new collared shirt he added to his work clothes, the clothes he wears to appear dependable, and invisible when needed. But he really isn't this conservative person—is he?—in pressed pants and shiny shoes, having an afternoon coffee with a dating-app woman.

He wonders what Rachel would think if she knew who he really is, deep down. Lisa claimed she did know who he was, at the beginning, but then left him for it, six years ago.

Since the divorce, Edward's been in therapy and read countless books about finding himself. He's Googled widely and deeply, read reams of comments from questioning people on Reddit, Quora, Wikipedia, and obscure sites he can't remember the names of, but none of them have told him who he is.

He peers through the passage toward the barista, who's wiping the counter and washing cups. She is trim and wiry, with a black apron over tight jeans and a brilliant gold shirt that's like a second skin. But when she turns and bends to fish something out of a bottom cupboard, he sees an outline of—could that be—male genitals? Is she not a woman, then? Or . . . He sits up straighter and squints. It's hard to tell from this distance. He leans forward, but then Rachel, coming back inside after her phone call, blocks his view.

"He's uncomfortable being alone, even though it's afternoon." She sits down but seems tense and doesn't pull the chair in.

Her son. "Will he be okay?" Maybe the storm feels a bit ominous to him, he thinks. He hopes Rachel might decide to leave, cut this thing short.

She takes a tiny sip of her drink, then sets it down again with a clatter.

"Is your coffee cold?" he asks. "I could ask them to warm it up."

She takes a deep breath in, then exhales. "Thanks, that would be nice."

He gets up, surprised, tired, and with what feels like growing dread, but smiles at her at the same time. She really is lovely, and she is obviously a concerned mother.

As he picks up her latté, the café lights spring on, catching the gold topaz in his ring—his ring from university—with a flick of fire. Perhaps that's an omen that things will get better with Rachel.

The mauve-blond barista is leaning back on the cupboard behind the counter, taking a breather. She watches him approach, her thumbs hooked into her pockets. Edward's body tenses under her gaze. She looks straight at Edward, waiting. Her eyes are brown-gold, catching the light of the pastry display case the way his topaz ring did.

"Could you warm this up, please?"

"Sure." A soft voice, but can he see a shadow along her jawline, next to the mauve hair?

"And, ah, maybe a couple of berry scones."

"Sure." She—they?—moves with quick efficiency, heating the latté and putting the scones together on a pretty, patterned plate. Edward decides "they."

"Ah, two plates, please. We're not together." Now why did he say that?

But they just smile, calm and sweet. "Okay, got it."

Edward's pressed black pants and beige shirt must scream uptight conservative. He tugs at his collar then pulls out his wallet. The way it slips into the palm of his hand gives him the strange sensation that it's something dangerous. As if he's pulled out a pistol. It's a very soft, expensive leather wallet full of cards. Dangerous in its own way, he thinks, and he has done well; he owns a five-bedroom house on Cumberland Street.

"Thank you, sir," the barista says when he pays.

The voice thrills him. *Sir.*

Back at the table, Rachel's phone is on the table again. He sees the blue of Messenger. He puts her mug and the plates down and sits. "A scone for you."

"*Scohhn?*" She draws out the 'oh' vowel as if she's never heard the word before. "I've always said *scahhn*, but I guess that's my Johannesburg upbringing."

"Oh . . ." Edward senses this is a correction and a criticism.

She is not easy to read. He decides to ignore it. "Do you go back much?"

"Once a year, to visit my parents." She pauses. "But not since Covid."

Edward nods. "That's hard," he says, an earnest empathy in his voice. For Edward, besides issues with his kids, Covid has revealed that he has no close friends. Pre-Covid, even the distant presence of Lisa and the kids in Halifax, and the steady stream of clients in his life, made it so he did not have to notice this.

Edward looks past Rachel and the *scahhns*, which neither of them has touched, to the barista again.

Finally, Rachel leans in to get his attention. "I must go. Yes." She nods. "Thank you very much, but I must go."

Edward hurries up the hill, his inadequate rain jacket zipped up as far as it can go, his tweedy, newsboy-style cap pulled down as far as it will go. When he's out in the daylight, the cap covers any possible roots or brassiness showing. For he has not let go of his own Havana Brown hair colour, and is committed to regular salon visits to maintain it. He's also dedicated to a dark weave—almost black—that he had his stylist work into the Havana Brown. No one seems to know he dyes his hair.

The wind is up, and he's wet and cold. Already, a few branches have broken from the trees; they lie in the grass around the town square. But what relief to be done with the coffee date. And when he's home, he can relax, loosen his thoughts.

Inside his front door, he pries off his shiny shoes and leaves them to drip-dry on the mat. He undresses in the laundry room, draping his wet clothes on the drying rack, and walks naked to his bedroom to put on jeans and a grey, long-sleeved T-shirt. Then it's back to the living room, where he uses the remote to turn on the propane fireplace.

NOT THE SAME ROAD OUT

He lies down on his white leather couch. Someone once called him a metrosexual.

Back before he met Lisa, he'd had a friend who'd called himself bigender.

Edward pulls his phone out of his pocket and searches: types of genders. A site pops up that identifies sixty-eight, then another site lists seventy-two. Really? He starts to read them, but he's hardly gotten out of the As and into the Bs when they all blur into one another. He can't track it all. It's overwhelming.

At least it's a relief to be warm, in his own house.

The friend's name was Oliver. And his last name? Oliver . . . something. Edward can't remember. But he remembers Oliver's dyed red hair, a short pixie cut, shaped sort of like the barista's, and he wore very bright colours—things like lime green jackets and pink suits—as well as metal jewellery, jagged earrings and sometimes eyeliner. He had the same slim, sinewy body as the barista, and a soft sweetness in his voice and smile. Again, like the barista. Oliver was an anthropology major, and he had wanted to share an apartment with Edward, he even loved to hike and bike the way Edward did, but Edward had gotten scared in the end, by Oliver's aura, energy, power, Edward never knew what to call it. He refused the offer and refused the friendship.

That energy. Soft, welcoming, but something lithe and vigorous underneath, a little mysterious or even dangerous. It made Edward want to get swallowed up in it.

He doesn't think anyone has ever thought of him as mysterious or dangerous. He values politeness, thoughtfulness. Recently, his daughter Fiona called him a people-pleaser. "And that's going easy on you," she added. "I could have said pathetic." This is the seventeen-year-old daughter he will be going to Halifax to "babysit" tomorrow, while Lisa is away.

But Edward doesn't want to think about whether he is pathetic or not. You have to people-please in real estate. He pulls the blanket off the back of the couch and covers himself with it. He ought to think about making himself dinner. But it's ridiculous, sitting solitary for dinner in this huge house. He bought it after the divorce and moved here thinking it would be perfect for Fiona and James, but they hardly come now.

The house would also be good for a partner in life, if he could only find one. Going online seemed his only option—he wasn't meeting anyone through his day-to-day doings. His clients range from fishers to farmers to senators and bankers, and lately, the Ontarians and Americans who've bought houses in the area. But you can't ask a client out for a date. He wouldn't cross that line.

You would think he'd have met someone in the community by now, though. He believes he's well thought of here. He's helping the town council develop plans for low-income housing. He gives generously to various non-profit programs, and he was thrilled to be part of supporting Syrian families emigrating to Nova Scotia. His BA in History included a minor in Ancient Mediterranean studies. He speaks French and knows some Arabic.

He became a realtor for the money, as an in-between thing, then it became permanent. Even so, his passion for history has helped in his real estate career. He tells his clients the histories of their houses, that Lunenburg was once called E'se'katik ("place of clams") by the Mi'kmaq, and he can tell tales about the rumrunners who used the coves and islands of the South Shore coast, back in the 1920s, to hide their alcohol-laden, bound-for-the-US ships. He has a good sense of the backgrounds of the various people he finds houses for, and he directs visitors with names like LeBlanc or Boudreau to Grand-Pré or other places where they can explore their Acadian roots. History's helped him in everything he's done in life. He's always told his kids this, though he doubts it has had much effect on them. His son James is a dancer—a *modern* dancer—very busy with life, and Fiona is a Greta Thunberg follower. Fiona thinks his generation has been a total failure.

Edward doesn't get around to making dinner. He falls asleep on the couch in front of the fire and wakes in the early hours of the morning feeling dehydrated, creaky, and annoyed with himself. Now he will feel tired for his visit to Halifax and seeing Fiona.

Edward has always been fascinated by the fact that the Magnetic North shifts; it can shift as much as 1,000 kilometres, due to movements in the Earth's magnetic core, which contains iron and nickel. Historically, the Magnetic North has moved around the Canadian north, but in recent decades, it seems to be moving towards Siberia. Edward wonders what Truth North Media might make of that scientific fact.

Though, like other orienteering enthusiasts, when he is out on the trails or travelling anywhere, he uses True North. It's what GPS systems use, it's what's on your phone, it's what Google uses.

In September 2019, True North and Magnetic North aligned at the Greenwich mean line for the first time in 360 years, though nothing dramatic happened as a result. Some people think the True North isn't a thing at all, that it's just a human-made dot on the map. Edward tends to agree, even though he is forced to use it.

When Edward arrives at Lisa's house in Halifax, Lisa has already departed. Fiona lets him in the front door without even saying hello, then flounces back to her bedroom.

Lisa's little spaniel, Cleo, dances around his feet and then rolls over for a tummy rub. "I'm glad someone is happy to see me," Edward says quietly, squatting down and stroking the dog's tummy.

It's Friday evening, what used to be Netflix-and-pizza night when Edward lived with Lisa and the kids. Edward puts his overnight bag in the guest bedroom, then goes and stands in the doorway of

SO LATE IN THE SEASON

Fiona's room. She's positioned herself in bed with the iPad that he bought her last Christmas balanced on her narrow knees. It blocks her face, and she doesn't move. Decidedly unwelcoming. He steps into the room a bit farther and notices that the cartoon-like eyebrows she had when he last saw her—GeoLift brows Lisa had told him—are now gone. That's a relief.

"What do you say, Sunshine, shall we order a pizza and watch a movie?"

She doesn't respond, just scowls into the iPad.

"Fiona," he tries again, thinking how stupid he was to call her Sunshine, his little-girl endearment from long ago. He keeps his voice soft—she should at least acknowledge him—"What would you like to do for dinner?"

"Mom left some soup for me."

"Oh . . . Okay . . ."

"I don't eat pizza."

"Oh . . ." This must be new, because at Lisa's bidding, he'd bought pizzas for Fiona's last birthday party, just a few months ago.

"I'll just eat it in here," Fiona says.

He had hoped to have some time watching a movie, sitting in the same room with her, at least. He wants to try again about that, but knows he'll get rebuffed.

"Dad . . . Edward!"

He looks up, realizes he's been staring at the floor. He hates it when she calls him that. The sentence that comes after it is bound to be awful.

"Why are you even here? I don't need a babysitter!"

"Well . . ."

"Mom just asked you because she feels sorry for you."

Ouch. Okay, there it is. He looks straight at her. "Now, that can't be true—"

"It is true!"

He pauses, touches the side of his head. "Oh, come on . . ."

"It's been true for as long as I've been on the planet," Fiona enunciates, delicately, distinctly. The words hang in the air.

"I think I'll sidestep that comment." He turns toward the door. "Since, I mean, perhaps, for the general purposes of—"

"Honestly, could you be more mealy-mouthed?" She sits up now, narrows her eyes at him, juts her chin out.

How has the daughter who used to delight in his attention, his Sunshine, come to despise him?

Her phone rings, and she adjusts to look at him side-eyed, eyebrows up, as if he's an imbecile. "I've got to get this," she enunciates, the way you might for someone who is hearing-impaired or a hundred years old.

He goes to the kitchen, his heart a tangle of embarrassment and pain. He heats up the soup, then takes a mug of it back to her, along with a chunk of bread, putting both on her bedside table as she talks to whoever it is.

Back in the kitchen, he sits down and tries to eat some of the soup himself, along with the bread, and some double brie he knows Lisa likely bought especially for him. Lisa had asked him to stay with Fiona and the dog just for the night, while she was on some work trip. Lisa had said she thought Fiona was stressed because James had got breakthrough Covid and was isolating in his apartment over near Dalhousie. Edward thought he was doing Lisa a favour. But now it dawns on him. What Fiona said is true: Lisa was doing him the favour.

There was a time when James and Fiona were interested in his orienteering hobby. He shared charts, compasses, an antique astrolabe that he's owned since he was a young man, and a quadrant with them. He showed them how to draw a compass rose with a pencil, drawing compass, and protractor. Edward also loves hourglasses, not the cheap ones you get for egg-timing or Boggle games, but ones that take an actual hour for the sand to run through. At home, he keeps a brass one on a hanging stand in his living room, and a more modern glass one that looks like a yin-yang symbol in his study.

Edward loves the idea that centuries ago, long before GPS and satellite systems, even before compasses, sailors used the sun and stars to navigate on the open seas. When James and Fiona were little, he taught them about ancient mariners who, in the northern hemisphere, used the North Star, or Polaris, to figure out what direction was north. That kept them from sailing in circles. If they could see Polaris, they knew how to stay on course.

Problems arose, though, when clouds obscured the stars' and planets' positions. This was the part of the story when Edward would bring out his compass. The first compass was probably invented in China, he told James and Fiona, then adopted in Europe somewhere in the twelfth century.

Fiona sits on her bed the whole evening, talking or texting friends on her various devices. Edward ends up in the living room, switching between CBC and CNN, then after a while he goes into Fiona's room again to retrieve the empty soup mug. She doesn't pay any attention to him. He notices for the first time that she's wearing sweats and looks unbathed. She smells like she's been rolling in carrots and whatever that smell is at health food stores. Turmeric? Edward thinks she looks pale and thin, too. He wonders if he ought to be worried; he'd thought Fiona was thriving.

After doing the dishes, he goes back to the living room and the TV. Lisa has arranged it so he'll leave tomorrow before she returns. He doesn't even know where she went, and now he realizes he's hurt that she didn't tell him, and that she didn't arrange it so they'd overlap. He likes to have check-ins with her. He's used to having her opinion on things. The debacle of Owls Head Park, for instance, global warming, Covid, the Islands exhibit at the gallery, her latest trail ride, the best kale salad recipe. Over the years, including the six since they were divorced, he's depended on her advice and capableness. And he wants an update on Fiona and details on the progress of James's Covid.

When he realizes he's no longer focusing on the TV, he powers it off.

In the marriage therapy Edward and Lisa had done, years ago, Lisa had spoken of emotional labour. He never grasped the exact meaning of that term. But one of her sentences was burned into his brain: "He won't take responsibility for his own nature."

Yet he felt as if he'd spent his entire life taking responsibility for it. His parents had taught him he must, if he wanted to be a happy, normal, accepted human being.

He and Lisa had met at a Y2K New Year's Party. (What a strange idea that seems now. Y2K! The digital dark ages!) But that night, just hours after meeting him, she'd asked him if he was gay. He'd said no. And he's never revealed to her—not then, not since—that from time to time, and especially back in high school, he'd wondered if he should be gay. But he's also been fine with women. He decided, if you're capable of going through life as a straight man, you might as well do so: be straight. You can avoid a lot of heartbreak that way, a lot of difficulty. And he has what he calls his rugged side; he's a cyclist and he lifts weights. He's often biked Rum Runners Trail between Halifax and Lunenburg, a round trip of 240 kilometres. When he was still married to Lisa and living in Halifax with her, they'd leave the kids with her sister and bike down to Lunenburg on a Saturday, stay over for dinner and a night at Bluenose Lodge, then bike back home the next day.

Edward has always rejected the idea that his "gender and

sexuality issues," as Lisa called them back then, had anything to do with their marriage problems. As long as he could conform to society's norms—and he was in fact attracted to women—where was the problem? He loved her. They had good sex. He was stable, financially successful, faithful, pleasant, a good dad, they had many shared interests, and he did everything he could to make her happy. Why wasn't that enough?

In the first years of using compasses, sailors noticed that their compass needles didn't always align with the North Star. They could see Polaris, but their compass didn't always point exactly north to it. This puzzlement went on for centuries, until the 1800s, when British scientists launched what became known as the Magnetic Crusade. They travelled around the world measuring what they called the "magnetic deviation," the difference between the Truth North of Polaris, and the Magnetic North of their compasses.

Edward ponders this as he drives back to Lunenburg the next day. His cell phone has both Google and Apple maps, and myriad trail and park apps, and when he travels abroad, he always elects to have a GPS in rental cars. But he knows that all these can fail. He is never without the backup of a compass and a paper map.

But none of this is helping him navigate his emotions. The drive home is painful. A cursory goodbye from Fiona, a mournful whine from Cleo, and here he is, hurtling along a slick Hwy 103—no abatement of the rain—and if he happened to die in a car accident, who would truly mourn the fact that he was gone? How long before anyone would even notice?

His parents moved to France decades ago, and he visits once a year in their new life, but they seldom talk on the phone and aren't big on email or even Facebook. He has no siblings, and he has not kept up with his cousins, none of whom live in Nova Scotia anymore.

He holds the steering wheel a little more tightly, vowing not to die on this car trip, but aware of some shadow self that wants to swerve the car into the ditch.

It's such a cliché to be thinking these thoughts, Edward admonishes himself. Of course he would not do anything that crazy.

That evening, back in his own house, he makes an omelet and a salad for his dinner, and realizes that, during his visit, he and Fiona spoke no more than, say, a hundred words altogether.

He tries a Netflix movie, choosing something folksy and a bit corny. Perhaps it will settle his nerves.

Before bed, brushing his teeth in front of the mirror, he has a sudden urge to cry. He allows his eyes to fill, then takes a towel and dabs at them. Despite the divorce, which he has always described as civil, organized, and fair, he loves Lisa. And, of course, he loves James and Fiona. Do they love him?

The next day, Saturday, is a busy one for real estate, and it's sunny and unseasonably warm. He calls Fern Realty and says he's under the weather. A colleague quickly agrees to cover for him for the weekend. In the ambiguous aftermath of Covid, no one is eager for your presence if you say you're under the weather. After ending the call, he goes back to sleep, then watches TV, consumes eggs, toast, apples, cheese, and many cups of tea, reads from his current book, *The Invention of Sicily,* as well as three stories from a Moroccan anthology Lisa lent him. He sleeps more, avoids his thoughts, keeps himself from calling Lisa.

He knows he ought to go out. The sun persists all day but has no effect on his cloistered mood. He looks at Rachel's profile a few more times on the app, then Googles her. He sees she studied architecture, something he hadn't seen on the app. Perhaps he ought to force himself to be more interested in her. But who knows if she is interested in him, anyway? The protocol of online dating exhausts him. It seems that, for him, it only leads to short, failed relationships.

But what if not calling her again hurts her feelings?

He goes to bed for the night with these uneasy thoughts, making it hard to fall asleep.

Sunday morning, Edward wakes early and gives himself a shake. A literal shake of his head and body, standing beside his bed, and then a few stretches. One day of wallowing is enough. He goes out to his garage, pulls his bike off its hook on the wall, and inflates the tires. Why hasn't he done a trail ride lately? He could go for a day-trip up Dynamite Trail to Chester today. As he searches for his bike helmet and gloves, he thinks that maybe next spring, he could plan a week-long bike trip on the Trans Canada Trail. Why not all the way up to Sydney Mines in Cape Breton? He has never gone that far. Probably he should find a biking buddy for such a trip. Not Lisa. Someone he has not yet met.

He takes the Bay to Bay trail that leads from Lunenburg to the town of Mahone Bay. It's only about ten kilometres, nothing for him despite the fact that he hasn't ridden much lately. After half an hour of gentle riding, he makes the turn onto Dynamite Trail at Repurpose Point, where there's an installation of repurposed historical industrial objects. This could not be more after his own heart. Iron pile rails from historical railway-building sites have been placed along the edges of the trail as benches. There are wharf bumpers from Lunenburg Harbour, old trawl and net anchors, an old excavator lattice, and a clam-shell bucket. Seventy-year-old, creosote-treated timbers from a nearby bridge. All with their own stories.

Dynamite Trail was so named because it used to be a CN rail corridor that brought dynamite to the wharf in Mahone Bay. When Edward gets on Dynamite Trail, he usually starts to travel faster on his bike, imagining his legs like the coupling rods on a train's wheels, strong and true and perfectly synced. He puts his head down and rejoices in his own power, tapping into some energy that seems to come from outside his body, but from inside it, too.

After a bit, Edward slows to a moderate speed. He knows he needs to pace himself. He may feel immortal now, but tomorrow his lower back and right knee may be speaking to him.

He glides by Oakland Lake on his left, then the little Commons Lake on his right, where there's a bench set in the trees. And then he is on the Narrows Basin Bridge—water stretching to both sides—and working his way up towards Martin's River.

It's an hour and a quarter since he left Lunenburg when he decides to turn off the trail and make his way down Martin's Point Road. He knows a place on the coast that's perfect for a rest and a snack. The road curls through some sweet houses. There's one he almost sold last year, but then the owners decided not to take the enormous sum being offered them. They stayed put. He thinks that was a good choice.

Edward follows the road as it circles down to the right. Then it reaches a bay where a row of small wharfs, made of boulders and timber, jut out into the Atlantic. Here, he swings off his bike and leans it against the seawall.

He stands on top of the boulders and looks out to the horizon, stretches his arms up, then spreads his legs too so that he is making a star shape. What a relief this feels in his body, how wonderful it is to open himself up to the sea and sky, and how supportive the ground feels below him. He feels the energy even through his biking shoes. Both the sun and a crescent moon greet him from opposite ends of the sky. They seem to accept him.

He pledges that tonight, before he goes to bed, he will go outside to observe the stars. That would be a lovely habit to cultivate.

He's brought two pieces of string cheese, a glass jar of trail mix, and a can of cold cider. He sits down cross-legged on a boulder to eat. The tide is moving out. He watches the horizon and devours his food, mixing the string cheese and raisin-filled trail mix in each bite—a satisfying blend of salt and sweet—then washes it down with a glorious stream of bright, sharp apple cider.

Gulls circle. One swoops in to sit on yet another boulder on his left, probably interested in his food. He closes his eyes, breathes all the way in, filling up every corner of his body before he slowly allows his breath to flow back out into the universe.

On Monday, the warm temperature continues. So strange.

He showers early and dresses, choosing sneakers, jeans, and a teal merino V-neck, and walks purposefully down the hill to Montague Street. It's just a few blocks. He takes two steps at a time up the front stairs of the coffee shop and turns left toward the counter. There's the Peter Pan hair, artfully messy this time, and the shiny elbows again. They're standing with their back to him, preparing something. There's just one group in the lineup in front of Edward this time.

"Oh, yesss . . ." He hears that soft voice again. "Mm-hmm."

"When did *you* leave?" The person standing closest to the counter is asking.

The barista turns. "Around midnight, I think. Everyone was still dancing . . ."

They're wearing a baggy grey T-shirt with the name of something on the front in cracked white letters. They have no makeup, a beard emerging out of the hint of shadow that Edward noticed last Thursday afternoon, and only one stud earring, with all the other holes leading up the sides of their ears empty. But Edward notes the same mauve nail polish, and possibly the same tight jeans.

They haven't noticed him. They're pouring frothed milk into a latté cup and continuing to answer questions about the night before.

When it's his turn, he feels a delighted fright that he hopes isn't visible. The barista smiles at him comfortably. Their choice to be manly today looks as natural as their choice to be womanly last Thursday.

Edward orders an oat milk chai, not his customary Americano. As he watches the barista prepare it, Edward reminds himself that this young person is not Oliver. And Oliver would be fifty-five by now, like Edward is, of course. Where would Oliver be living now, and what would he be doing? Perhaps Edward ought to find out. More to the point, though, is what would Edward be doing now if he'd said yes to rooming with Oliver way back then.

Edward chooses the tiny one-person table in the corner this time, near the barista's counter. There, glancing up occasionally, he sips his drink and, spurning emails or the news, reads an article about the El Gusto Orchestra of Algiers on his phone.

He speaks to no one but observes the barista when he can. And when he's done, Edward says a polite goodbye.

Out on the street again, the breeze feels light on his cheeks. He walks up the hill through the town park, toward home. It's remarkable. Unseasonably warm.

His heart feels tender. Two women pass him with adorable dogs on leashes. One is a spaniel, like Lisa's.

He hasn't gotten an update on James yet and he experiences a sudden stab of fear. *Is* James going to be okay? Dear, sweet, dancing James. And, he wonders, is James like him? Fluid? Bigender? Or any of the seventy other possibilities, according to the web? Well, of course he is. And why has Edward never addressed this? He's known for all of James's twenty years that he was not your usual boy, not "hetero-normal" (that terrible word). Edward makes a vow to learn about all the genders and sexualities there are out there, and if James is open to it, talk to his son about it.

When he gets home, he'll call James, then put music on and just bliss out lying on his living room floor. And, for now, he thinks, he'll go gentle with Fiona, wait until she likes him again.

A gust of wind lifts the elm branches above, and autumn yellow leaves flutter down all around him, like confetti. It's as if he's at some special private wedding to himself.

At the edge of the park, his eye is caught by a hedge that's burst into unusual colour. Maybe the warm spell has tricked it into blooming. He stops to check it out. He doesn't know the name of it, but he sees that the leaves swaying in the wind have given birth to flowers.

He bends over them: tight, dark-purple flowers that have freakishly—no, tenderly—bloomed, so late in the season. It's as if the sun has helped them discover an extra life to inhabit, to rejoice in.

Movie Night

TRACY KREUZBURG

Newfoundland and Labrador | Corner Brook Connector

She was so skinny you could have seen the sins on her soul, if she had any. The pretty brunette with long, straight hair, a teenager, watched Mr. Bellows through the window of the green clapboard store. The man was smiling as he hauled several long, scrodded benches from the back room of the building into the open floor space. You could see the track marks worn into the faded linoleum from the repeated back-and-forth dragging of the beaten-up old pews. The girl's eyebrows were slightly scrunched, her thin lips pursed, as she tapped impatient fingers on her leg. Inside, the storekeeper flicked the switch between the large front window and the solid, grey-painted door, and a single light illuminated the Bellows General Store, drawing in the moths for their nightly scuff about the tungsten filaments.

    She wasn't alone. A dozen or so teenagers were gathered on the side of the dirt road that hugged the shoreline of Mount Moriah, buzzing like the candle chasers bopping around the store light. It was a beautiful September evening, maybe a little too warm because the flies were bothersome, though not so warm as to quash the pleasant breeze off the water, nor dull the ditzy blue glitter created when the setting sun's last rays hit the ripples. The fragrance of the large lilac tree sitting in the Powers' yard across the street competed

MOVIE NIGHT

with the salty smell of the waves on the water side of the road. But the young folks were oblivious, antsy to get into the shop. Even though the OPEN sign was hanging in the picture window, its glass slightly cracked and taped at one corner, they all knew the door was locked for about fifteen minutes at a quarter to seven every Friday evening.

Shell was feeling nervous because Terry hadn't arrived yet. She was also anxious because a different boy had just joined the gaggle waiting for the door to open. "Gert," she whispered to her best friend, "Stop moving so much. I need to keep behind you so Keith doesn't look at me. I'll just die if he says something to me!"

Gert rolled her eyes but stood in place, between Shell and Keith King, who'd been Shell's steady throughout the school year. Keith had gone away to Toronto to work for the summer. He'd written her some letters, but as August approached, she started to date Terry, who'd had a crush on her since Grade 6. Shell and Terry spent a lot of time together over the summer with their friends, swimming in Tuck-In Brook, sun-tanning on the wharf, and sneaking a few of Amos's father's homebrew to drink in The Spot in the backwoods. Shell was fourteen and a half years old, and a whole summer felt like forever to wait around for Keith, even though he had just graduated from high school and had his own car.

Keith's father and sister had picked him up from the CN bus in Corner Brook on Labour Day. Though the railway was still operating, most everyone was taking the bus across the island now because it was quicker.

"Faster than the Newfie Bullet. Hated travelling that train to work when I was your age," Mr. King said as he shook his son's hand. He then complimented him on how well his moustache had grown in. Before he had a chance to complain about how long his son's curly brown hair had gotten, Wanda jumped in. "Your sweetheart and Terry Brake are dating now, ya know," she said with a smirk. Keith stayed quiet, lowered his eyes, and then stared out the window as his father drove. He was hurt and upset, not willing to admit or show it to his sister or his dad. *That Terry, he's going to pay up.* Brooding on the drive home to Mount Moriah, Keith decided he couldn't go to his old school to cause a ruckus. After all, he wasn't a kid anymore, and he wanted to make sure Terry knew that. The truth was that Keith felt humiliated. He was a man now, and while he was away working, a *boy* stole his girlfriend. He couldn't *not* kick his arse.

Shell was relieved when Mr. Bellows finally had the projector set up inside. He took a handkerchief sticking out of his overalls pocket and wiped the sweat dripping from his thinning, grey hair. He shoved it back in his pocket and then opened the door so the lot of them could rush the counter to buy drinks and claim the brown paper bag of salted popcorn the shopkeeper gave the kids. Then, as per the normal routine, he called out, "Tony and Phil, go pin up the big screen on the wall, but keep it a bit farther from the cash register than last week." Together, the two tallest boys in the room approached the store counter; each took an end of a double-size sheet and pinned it high on the wall with a few thumbtacks.

The chattering crowd started taking their seats on the benches, with the smell of Coke and buttery popcorn filling the warm space. Friday night was the only time Bellows General Store shed its usual aromas of cardboard and flour, allspice and tobacco smoke. From the corner of her eye, Shell saw Keith watching her and was relieved when Terry walked through the door, a smile appearing on his face as soon as his eyes found her. She waved and called out, "Here!" pointing to the open space she saved for him, next to where she and Gert sat. Keith slumped on a bench two rows behind, sitting with Mike and Jerry, who would be graduating this year. The back of Shell's head felt hot, burning from his eyes staring at her. When Terry put his arm around her shoulders, she felt as if everyone in

MOVIE NIGHT

the room was watching them—and Keith. She was happy when Mr. Bellows finally turned off the lights, hiding the blazing blush that was creeping up her freckled cheeks.

Then, as the kids quieted and the sound of crinkling paper bags filled the makeshift theatre, Amos, as loudmouthed as he was short, called out, "So what's we watchin' tonight, Mr. Bellows?" Grinning, the shopkeeper said, "You'll find out. Just keep yer pants on, son." A few laughs erupted among the teenagers focused on the 250-thread-count cotton movie screen as numbers flashed and rolled backwards, and theme music started to play. They all clapped as *The Love Bug* lit up the sheet. The movie was probably three years old already, but many in the group rarely got to the Majestic movie theatre in Corner Brook and had only ever watched the movies shown at the store. Shell was one of the few who'd already seen *The Love Bug*, but she wasn't going to say so.

It had been Mr. Bellows' idea to set up movie night at his store. He said there wasn't much for the young folks to do on a Friday evening besides getting into trouble, and he wanted to give them something fun. Since he started the regular evening, every parent in Mount Moriah knew where their teenager was at 7:00 pm on Friday night.

Gert leaned into Shell and said, "Dean Jones is sooo handsome," sighing dramatically.

"Sure is." Shell thought Jones wasn't anything like as handsome as her heartthrob, Elvis Presley. When she had seen them on the screen together in *Jailhouse Rock*, she didn't rate him at all. Gert was also an Elvis fan, but not nearly as devoted as Shell, who wore a white silky scarf tied around her neck, like those Elvis often wore. Gert, who wore her long, dark blond hair up in a ponytail, was more concerned that the ribbon in her hair matched her outfit. Tonight, it was red, the same as her shorts.

The movie was almost two hours long, and aside from a trip to the bathroom, and despite repositioning her behind repeatedly on the hard wooden bench, Shell's whole body was feeling sore and stiff, so she popped up from her seat before the credits started to roll. Even Gert must have been relieved when Herbie drove off with Jim and Carole for their honeymoon, as she too stood up and clapped loudly.

Chatter erupted as the teenagers started to make their way out of the store, thanking Mr. Bellows on the way out.

"See you two later," Gert said, waving at Shell and Terry as she turned and headed toward the path to her house on the side of a hill near the store. Then Shell remembered Keith. Tugging Terry's arm, she tried to whisk him away, but he had already locked eyes with her old boyfriend, and suddenly everyone still standing at the side of the road was quiet. Her stomach started to turn, and she was afraid she would vomit partly digested popcorn over the brown-and-white saddle Oxford shoes she'd borrowed from Gert.

"No, no, no," she said meekly as Terry moved her toward Amos and his other buddies, knowing there was nothing she could do now to stop whatever was about to happen. Terry and his friends were two years younger than Keith, but most of Keith's friends had moved out of town after high school. Keith was bigger and likely stronger, thought Shell, but Terry had more back-up if needed. But Keith looked really angry, as if he didn't even notice anyone but Terry.

"I should fuckin' kill you," Keith shouted at Terry, lunging and landing a right hook squarely under his chin. Shell watched in horror as blood poured from Terry's mouth over his big collar shirt, and he stumbled back with a dazed look in his eyes. Keith didn't get the chance to throw another punch. Terry's eyes rolled up, and he hit the ground hard, his head landing on a small boulder. Someone screamed, though it wasn't Shell. Shocked, she watched more blood oozing from Terry, now from the back of his blond head, soaking into the gravel.

MOVIE NIGHT

She heard Keith say, "Shit." Amos ran into the store. Shell saw Mr. Bellows pick up the phone and dial hurriedly. After a short call, he hung up and mouthed what Shell assumed was a string of curse words. He started to dial again as Amos anxiously stood next to him. Shell took the white scarf from her neck, balled it up, and knelt beside Terry, gently lifting his head and placing it under him as a cushion. The white silk turned crimson, but seemed to slow or stop the bleeding, or at least Shell hoped so. Keith paced back and forth while nervously running his fingers through his curly hair, stopping frequently to call out, "Terry, c'mon, c'mon, get up, b'y."

A couple of minutes that felt like twenty passed before Mr. Bellows and Amos came out of the store. The storekeeper looked at Terry lying motionless on the dirt road and spoke sternly, loudly, not sounding like himself at all. "I called Doc Matthews, he's home and he lives just up from the bank in Curling. He'll be waiting for you outside and said to bring him right away." The way he said it made it clear to everyone how serious the situation was.

"Jerry, come help me get him into my car!" Keith shouted. Amos ran ahead and yanked open the backseat door. Jerry sat on the back seat and scooched in with his hands under Terry's armpits, while Keith held onto his lower body. Amos ran to the other rear door and opened it so Jerry could ease out of the car, making sure Terry's head was carefully positioned on the seat. Keith then gently bent his legs to fit him comfortably inside. Keith's face had drained of all colour, and he breathed quickly as he repeatedly squeezed the back of his neck. He turned to Shell, nodded, and said, "C'mon, get in."

Shell slid into the familiar passenger seat of Keith's blue Chevy sedan, leaving her bloodied scarf on the ground, and turned around to look at Terry lying across the back seat, still unconscious. She realized she must have started bawling at some point, and used the back of her hands to wipe the mascara from her face. Keith started the car and hit the gas, leaving the shocked onlookers in a huge,

NOT THE SAME ROAD OUT

blinding cloud. As the cloak of sandy dust surrounded them, like a dry-ice fog, and flowed through the car's open windows, they might have been in a movie themselves. Shell tasted sand in her mouth.

Travelling through and past Mount Moriah, they approached the blind turn just outside the road into Curling. Overcome by fear and urgency, Keith did not slow down, and Shell did not ask him to. By the time they saw a chocolate brown horse and her cocoa-coloured foal crossing the road, it was too late. Shell screamed and covered her face as the car struck hard. The mare hit the windshield, and the little foal exploded over the front of the car. From the backseat, Terry mumbled, "Whaa . . . "

Now blood splatter joined the road grit inside the car. Keith and Shell were as still as crash-test dummies for several long moments. Then Keith lifted his hands from the wheel and watched them shake. Shell took her hands down slowly from her face, turned to Keith and said, "Are you okay?" Seeing the horrified look on his face, she lifted her hand to her hair and felt sick as her fingers came away covered with blood and stickiness. "Don't worry, I'm okay, Keith! It's not my blood," she said as her bottom lip trembled.

After taking a few slow, shuddering breaths, Keith nodded and got out. He walked around the crushed front of his car to the other side. The passenger door was jammed, so he helped Shell climb out of the window. Keith then stood still for a moment. "I don't feel hurt. How could I not be hurt?" Shell pushed past him and opened the back door. Terry was trying to sit up. Keith and Shell helped him out, each taking an arm over their shoulders and guiding him to a nearby cherry tree. They helped him sit on the ground, and he leaned heavily against it, but didn't seem to have any new injuries.

"You stay here, and I'll go get someone," said Keith as Shell gently touched different parts of Terry's body. Seemingly oblivious, she asked Terry, "Do your legs or arms hurt?" As Keith was leaving, he heard Terry say no, and Shell said, "Keith's gone for help." But

MOVIE NIGHT

someone had already heard the crash and was running toward them from one of the nearby biscuit box houses. It was Gussy Brake, a friend of Keith's father.

He looked over at the crushed car, the boy leaning against the tree, the girl with blood in her hair, the shaky teenager, and said, "Keith b'y, you take my truck and get that one to the doctor. I'll call the police and get them over here. I lost me cousin out east in Port Blanford when the causeway washed out a few years ago. It's only right to help people ya knows are in trouble."

"Thanks so much," said Keith. As Shell was about to speak, Mrs. Brake appeared with a small pile of towels and rags and a jug of water. "Now don't worry, I've gone ahead and called the police, so you get him to the doc's place."

"Yes," said Gussy. "I'd take you meself, but me eyes aren't the best for night driving these days."

Back at the tree, Shell gently cleaned Terry's head and told him to hold a cloth against the gash. She wiped dried blood from his mouth, glad his lip had stopped bleeding, though she noticed a gap where a tooth was missing. Then she wiped as much of the foal's bloody insides off her head as she could manage while Keith and Gussy helped Terry into the truck. Shell got into the driver's side of the truck and slid across to sit beside her boyfriend.

The three teenagers, all with a smattering of red splayed over them, sat in a row. Shell turned to her right and asked, "What's your full name?"

"Terrence Rufus Buckle."

"What's your address?"

"Box 77, Mount Moriah, Newfoundland."

"What's today's date?"

"September 10th"

"Good, good," said Shell.

Keith looked at her quizzically.

"My little sister had seizures when she was eight, and those were the same questions I asked her when she came to. My aunt is a nurse and told me to ask questions like that if Claire has a seizure, and also if someone bangs their head hard."

"So this means Terry should be okay then?" He didn't look at Shell as he asked.

"I hope so." Like Keith, she looked straight ahead as the headlights forced themselves through the blackness and into bright, misshapen blobs on the gravel.

No one had anything to say, and only the sound of the engine and the tires on the road filled Gussy's truck. Shell started to notice her breathing again, and her heart beat more slowly. She glanced at Terry, who looked shattered. He groaned softly but was still awake. Then she started to cry again.

"S'alright, Shell. We're almost there," Keith said.

But she was thinking about the poor mama horse and baby horse, and their guts splattered over the car and the road. She thought about having to explain to the doctor what had happened, and then to her parents when she got home afterward. She thought about the car that Keith's dad had fixed for him for his graduation, now a write-off. She worried that Terry probably had a fractured jaw and had been unconscious for a long stretch of time. Was he going to be okay? What about brain damage? Shell knew that everyone down the bay, in Mount Moriah, Curling and maybe even Corner Brook, and everyone at school, would know everything before the night was out. Would she be blamed for it all? Should she be blamed? She closed her eyes tightly and willed the tears to stop flowing.

Keith, eyes still on the road, winced at each pothole the truck hit. He cleared his throat. "Terry, I'm sorry, man. Real sorry." Shell and Terry knew he wasn't talking about the rough bumps, but neither said anything.

"I know, b'y." Terry looked over at Keith and Shell. Keith's face

MOVIE NIGHT

was a mass of dark red spots, ghostly pale underneath. Shell's eyes were puffy and red, and he could see spots of dried blood she'd missed when she cleaned herself. Terry could tell she was all shook up by how tightly her jaw was clenched, just like other times when she was upset. He often teased her about this, but this wasn't the time. He looked away from them both, to the road, and said quietly, "Thanks for taking me to the doctor. Sorry about your car."

Shell closed her eyes, felt her shoulders drop and let out a very long breath she hadn't realized she'd been holding. Terry touched one of the hands she was holding tightly together on her lap. He saw that some colour was coming back into Keith's face as he pretended not to look and turned up the radio. "Stuck in the Middle with You" by Stealers Wheel was playing. Shell *almost* chuckled.

It was a long time before she went to another movie night.

The Light in the Sky

SHARON HUNT

Quebec | Parc Linéaire des Bois-Francs, La Traversée de Charlevoix

> "Behold, I shew you a mystery; . . . we shall all be changed . . . in the twinkling of an eye, at the last trumpet . . . this mortal must put on immortality.
> 1 CORINTHIANS 15:51-53

It is Sunday and we are leaving by nine, if my father moves around faster, but on weekends, he likes to sleep in. Since my mother's death, he wakes, rolls over in their double bed and checks the light in the sky. If it is bright, he gets up quickly, remembering her chastisement to stop being so lazy; if the light is hazy and she is quiet, he sleeps another hour.

The light this morning is hazy.

Blessedly, though, the air feels like rain. We need it. The lake is a foot lower than normal in August, and there is a water ban rendering the roses and azaleas corpses and the grass dust, if you look at it sideways, my father likes to say.

According to him, if you look at anything "sideways," something bad will happen. It's an old superstition handed down from his mother, who received it from her own, and he says it because it reminds him of her.

Someone or something has been looking at the forests sideways because they are burning, although that is because of the negligent forest management, not climate change, he insists and, finally, the experts are telling politicians that they have ruined the forests with their stupid rules and regulations.

My father is happy that people are growing spines again.

Max Hastings, the university professor who moved his wife and four children onto our crescent three years ago, refuses to speak to my father anymore because of his climate opinions. Max even denounced him and them as "ridiculous, dangerous, completely unacceptable."

"Thomas Hunter should be locked away," Max has said.

To a one, our longstanding neighbours have defended my father.

"Old people are being pushed around too much now and we have had enough," Mr. Cotter, from the bungalow at the end of our crescent, told Max.

Mr. Cotter, a retired professor whose specialty was the Anglo-Saxons, also told him to "shove off" and in their last come to, when Max strode away shouting that there were no such things as Anglo-Saxons, Mr. Cotter countered, "but there are such things as pricks, and you are a prime example of one."

Mr. Thompson, our next-door neighbour, told us that he had to run into the house because he was laughing so hard he pissed his pants.

Shortly afterward, the Hastings' two-storey, yellow brick went up for sale but so far there have been no viewings.

Mr. Thompson laments that "if Max is so hell bent on helping the climate, he should have installed triple-pane windows and a heating pump like the three of us did."

By the three of us, he means himself, my father, and Mr. Cotter, who have become something of a Three Musketeers for the elderly lot.

"And he and his wife are still driving around in gas-guzzling behemoths," my father added.

Mr. Thompson has even less use for Max than we did because

when Elaine Thompson died last year, "Max came over and asked if I was going to sell now that my wife was gone, since the house was too big for one person and he knew someone who would take the place, sight unseen."

"He was lucky he was not seen off with a good right cross. John Thompson was once a Golden Gloves champion and went to the Olympics," my father reminded me.

My father, too, knows a bit about boxing, having been taught by his father for self-defence as a child.

Since Max's attacks, Mr. Thompson and Mr. Cotter have kept my father company many evenings in the porch, over single malt whisky and roast beef sandwiches that I have waiting for them in the refrigerator.

All three men are tall and still sturdy, if a bit stooped. Mr. Thompson is a gardener, while Mr. Cotter, a distance runner, has thrice competed at Boston. My father loves to walk and became an avid biker after my mother died, developing an interest in biking sections of the Trans Canada Trail, particularly those in Quebec, a province he has fallen in love with over decades of travelling through it.

This morning, we are heading to Quebec again and onward to the east coast, and I am in the sun porch to turn off the radio and check that the doors to the deck are locked. My father sometimes forgets the doors now and always leaves the radio on when he goes to bed because he likes to hear other voices in the morning. He imagines my mother and a neighbour sitting and chatting over coffee. Of course, they never are and never were because she was not one for inviting neighbours over to chat. Chatting always led to gossip, and she grew up around women "who ripped the flesh from your bones" in that regard.

Leaving the radio on is just a comfort, he assures me, nothing to worry about.

THE LIGHT IN THE SKY

Hardly dangerous I told myself, when it began a year ago but, along with the occasional unlocked door, there have been other things that have grown increasingly alarming.

During the week, he is up first because I work late. As a medical textbook editor, I can concentrate better when he has gone to bed. On weekends, I am first out of bed and turn off the radio, like my mother would have, if he had ever left it on when she was alive.

We do not waste.

While admirable, her constant hectoring about a light on in the hall or a piece of cheese in the garbage was oppressive, as if such things would lead to eternal darkness and famine, when our money ran out.

When, not if, she always said, although our money never ran out in her lifetime and, I am sure, will not in my father's or mine. There has been a lot of money for decades because he has been a very good investor, buying blue-chip stocks that are now worth a fortune. Plus, he paid off the mortgage years ahead of time from working at the same job at the nylon plant for forty years, retiring with a good pension, too.

My work pays well and, since moving back into the family home after my mother's death, I have not had rent expenses and, like him, invest wisely.

We're as rich as Rockefeller. He'd say that to make her laugh and stop worrying, although she rarely did either.

This morning, organ music on the radio is quickly drowned out by the Reverend Jim Turner, pastor of the Church of Almighty Love, in some southern town whose name is obliterated by sudden crackling.

When the crackling clears, Reverend Jim is reciting First Corinthians, which I know by heart because it is my father's favourite Bible verse, something he has recited often.

As if on cue, he appears in the porch as the Reverend thumps on something, "at the last trumpet."

"Behold, I shew you a mystery," my father says, in a deep baritone not unlike Reverend Jim's, except without the southern twang, although still with a subtle Irish one, indicative of Newfoundlanders.

Moving to Ontario in the 1960s, he did his best to get rid of it. Being a Newfoundlander in Ontario then was a ponderous burden of Newfie jokes and references to brothers sleeping with their sisters and other offensiveness that today would be called out as racism. Then, though, if you got upset over such things, you were told to get a sense of humour.

Sometimes, you were told that "You're lucky we let the lot of you become part of the country, otherwise, you would be more ignorant than you already are."

He heard that sometimes at work but walked away, refusing to allow some ignoramus to drum him out of his job.

I heard another version of it from my Grade 6 teacher, after I told the principal that she had thrown a boy across the classroom because he had not memorized "The Raven."

"You Newfies are all stupid troublemakers," she said, after cornering me in the hall.

"I was born in Ontario."

"The blood's still running thick through you."

After that, I stayed mute, not telling my parents because my mother would say I was too clever by half and should have minded my own business, and my father would have kept the peace by agreeing with her.

When that teacher died, I doubted that she would be changed "in the twinkling of an eye."

My father repeats those words and the rest of First Corinthians again, now. They float off his tongue, unimpeded by much of a twang or an old stutter that resurfaces if he is tired or overwrought.

He holds "immortality" fast for five beats before switching off the radio.

THE LIGHT IN THE SKY

Sighing, he closes his eyes for an instant, no doubt thinking about his two boyhood friends, John and Donald (coincidentally, Mr. Thompson and Mr. Cotter's first names), for whom First Corinthians gave them the courage to carry out the plan the two of them had agreed.

When he opens his eyes, he says, "Will we get going home?"

"Yes."

Although he has lived more of his life here—in this Ontario city of limestone and prisons—he still refers to that spit of an island off Newfoundland's Avalon coast as home, although he turned his back on it at seventeen.

Mr. Cotter is from Ontario, but Mr. Thompson is also an East Coast boy, from Nova Scotia, moving here around the same time as my father to avoid becoming another sacrifice for the sake of coal. In my father's case, it was an iron ore mine he avoided, although his father and uncles worked in it all their lives, then died from emphysema or bronchitis that "caught their breath and refused to give it back."

"I wanted to breathe as long as I could," he says, if talking of his youth.

Breathless after carrying his suitcases out to the car, he gives Mr. Thompson a house key to check on things for the three weeks we will be gone. Mr. Cotter left earlier this week for his cottage or he would have gotten a key as well.

It has been eight years since my father and I visited Newfoundland together, although he has taken two trips on his own in that time, each with extended stays in Quebec to visit friends and bike more of the trails.

Before we leave this morning, he insists I take a photograph of him and Mr. Thompson standing side by side, almost touching but with a thread of light between them. He never wants his picture taken. Like me, he does not like to look at himself, in a photograph or in a mirror, although for obvious reasons the mirror is unavoidable. A photograph is not, yet here he stands, beside his friend, awaiting the snap of my digital camera.

I feel embarrassed by the request, although I cannot say why, but take two photographs before asking them to put an arm around each other's shoulder. They demure and the session is over.

"Bring him back safely," Mr. Thompson says, then straightening, smiles.

"Both of you back safely, of course, I mean," he adds, before walking back up his driveway. He turns to wave when my father calls out, "See you in time, John."

"Yes, Tom, in time."

As I wait for the traffic to clear on Lakeside Drive, my father tunes in again to Reverend Jim who is ending his service as it began, with First Corinthians. My father repeats his story about the young John and Donald's love of that verse but says nothing of his shame at having deserted them when they needed him the most. He does not have to because the shame is always in his voice and eyes when he speaks of those long-dead boys.

On Lakeside, he sits up straighter, eyes wide open. He was born within the sight of an ocean and is bereft when he is not near water, which is why he spent much more than he could afford forty years ago for our two-storey house because it backs onto the lake that, on most summer mornings, looks like a silver thread, from our deck.

This morning, that thread unwinds to our left, as the road undulates. Soon, there will be only occasional glimpses of water until we get to the ocean, so he is drinking in the sight of it and hoping the memory will be a balm when he is parched from nothing but dusty fields and yellowing trees.

When we get onto the highway, he settles back for a nap that lasts four hours, until I nudge his arm and say, "Quebec ahead."

THE LIGHT IN THE SKY

He sits up, smiles.

"*Je me souviens.*"

Quebec is his favourite part of the trip. Outside of Montreal, highways curl and rise, fall and straighten, pass green and lush farmland and the silvered steeples of towering churches. Lakes appear, as cold and deep as oceans, hedged by swaths of forest that stretch beyond the horizon. Great spans of iron bridges offer glorious vistas, and beyond Quebec City's ancient cobblestones, the St. Lawrence River whips up whitecaps or moves along, blue, shimmering and calm.

The people, older Québécois mostly, that he has met over the decades have always been kind. Some are kindred spirits who share not only his hurt over humiliations endured at the hands of Ontarians, but who are generous in sharing food, conversation and a love of the outdoors, something that has sustained my father through his years in Ontario.

"I like to think of myself as an adopted son," he said, when we were last in Quebec.

"An Anglo, but allowed."

We laughed.

Still, the thought filled him with pleasure.

He has often talked about buying a little place up toward Quebec City. There would be more time to walk and bike the trails not yet crossed off his list, but he would miss Mr. Thompson and Mr. Cotter too much to do this yet.

Still, he feels more at home in Quebec than in Ontario or even Newfoundland. Quebec gives him an energy and passion that is quickly siphoned away in other places.

Now, crossing the border, he says, "Watch for a Couche-Tard."

It must be a Couche-Tard convenience store because he loves the winking red owl on the sign. Quickly finding one, we stop for coffee, crullers, and ham and cheese sandwiches.

NOT THE SAME ROAD OUT

I packed a lunch to get us through our first day but, like a child, he insists on buying food and sitting outside, his right leg over his left and swinging, eating off cardboard plates.

He returns to the store for chocolate bars and a magazine, which he flips through on the way to the car, then passes on to me.

"The type is too small," he says.

"Your eyesight is perfect."

He laughs and puts his arm around my shoulder.

"I really bought it for you, my genius girl."

For a moment, I think of warning him not to continue down the road that starts and ends with a long-ago IQ test that branded me a genius, and the tester who confessed to my parents in an almost reverential tone that he had never encountered anyone with a 182 IQ, and a girl, in Grade 4, no less. He then insisted I should be advanced three grades, but my mother said she did not want me to stand out from my classmates.

Even knowing how much I wanted to advance, my father agreed with her and I stayed put, bored and fuming.

This is the one thing for which I have never forgiven him because I think my life would have turned out differently had I been allowed to stand out. I might have become a doctor instead of editing textbooks for those training to be, but I lost heart and interest in school after Grade 4, and after high school went to a community college instead of university because I no longer wanted to stand out.

Still, I let the genius girl comment pass, not wanting to spend the rest of the day with him in a sulk.

Before we leave this Couche-Tard, he stands with the red owl over his shoulder for a photograph. He wants me to "take lots of pictures, to remember this trip."

Saying this, he seems on the verge of tears.

"I'll get them printed when we get back, and we can make an album to show Mr. Thompson and Mr. Cotter."

THE LIGHT IN THE SKY

He smiles then, his lovely, broad smile of my childhood Christmas mornings, as I marvelled at books and toys, CD players and Polaroid cameras.

We follow the Autoroute 40 through Montreal's perpetual construction and later merge onto one of the highways that eventually leads to Nova Scotia and the overnight ferry to Port aux Basques. From there it will be another eight hours to St. John's and an hour further to the cove and a smaller ferry to the island, where we will stay with Clyde, my father's brother who, like him, is a widower.

I am an only child, but Clyde has seven who fled Newfoundland for the Alberta oilfields and enough money to feed whatever addictions developed. For Stephen, the eldest, who saved me from drowning when I first visited, the addiction is Oxy, prescribed after he injured his back. Stephen is living again with his father, who is trying to straighten him out.

Clyde himself is an alcoholic, so my father is not optimistic that he will succeed.

The island—all we ever call it—was once awash with Hunters, among the first to row across the strait between the main island of Newfoundland and this small rock two hundred years ago. Now, there are only a few second and third cousins, as well as Clyde and Stephen, remaining. The rest are either in Ontario, Alberta or Texas, many lured south by the dream of black gold and wealth.

As we head north, we frequently pull into rest stops with their square brick washrooms and picnic tables under trees.

"We'll spend tonight at the Bon Jour Motel and see Mr. Bouchard?"

My father shrugs.

Other times, this would have been a given. Yves Bouchard, the motel owner, is also an avid biker who has spent many days on nearby trails with my father.

Today, his nonchalance is upsetting but still, I take the exit to the motel. As we near, its green and pink paint looks cheery, but up close, the Bon Jour is tired and worn out, like we are at the end of this first day.

It's clear the motel has fallen on hard times since I was last here, although my father has said nothing about any problems. He and Mr. Bouchard exchange birthday and Christmas cards, but thinking back, I realize I didn't see a Christmas card last year.

The paint on the motel's cabins is peeling, with thick ribbons of it littering the pitted asphalt. The office still has its plastic dancer in the window, but part of the welcome sign—*Ici tu es chez toi*—has burnt out, leaving only the first two words illuminated. The diner, which seemed always busy, is deserted. A waitress crouches outside, smoking, but when she sees our car, stands, and sashays away.

On our last visit, we stayed an extra day so we and Mr. Bouchard could bike the Bois-Francs Linear Park path. We brought our bikes, expensive Japanese models that for the last two years have rarely left the garage, and the next morning, the three of us followed the old railway line, biking under canopies of trees, mesmerized by the breathtaking views. At lunch, we sat on a hill overlooking a low-lying plain to enjoy the sandwiches and cheese and a good bottle of wine that Mr. Bouchard had packed for us.

The ride back was filled with joking and laughter, even when it started to rain. For the first time since my mother's death, my father looked truly happy.

That evening, he ticked off the Bois-Francs ride and studied the map for the next adventure.

Mr. Bouchard suggested that the trail up around Charlevoix would be a good choice, but only my father and I have travelled it in summer so far.

Now, looking around at the plastic planters with their plastic tulips and the sagging bucket chairs, my father shakes his head.

THE LIGHT IN THE SKY

"We would be better sleeping in the car, even if that bear is waiting to come back and do more than pass by, this time."

"That bear? That was thirty years ago," I blurt, adding, "I'm not sleeping in the car and I'm not driving any farther today."

"Thirty years ago. It was just last week. Ask your mother, she will set you straight."

Realizing what he has said, he stares straight ahead, his bottom lip trembling.

We sit silently, watching a man get out of a truck and carry black garbage bags into Number 3, then my father taps my shoulder.

"I was only joking. I know the bear's not in Quebec. Never mind, I will get us a room."

While he is gone, I cry, no longer able to dismiss the fact that something is going wrong with my father's memory. His mother was diagnosed with dementia around his age and, while he refuses to believe that will ever happen to him, I think it is and has been happening for a while.

Sometimes, he wakes me in the night to say goodbye before heading off to work, and it takes my repeated assurances that he has been retired for over a decade to lure him back to his bed.

In May, I found him kneeling on his bathroom vanity, slapping at the shaking mirror. When I asked what he was doing, he said he was trying to free the boys behind it.

"Can't you see, they're scared and crying."

Then, like that, he climbed down and walked past me, laughing.

"I got you, didn't I?"

He is laughing now as he returns to the car, waving a key attached to a piece of wood shaped like a tree. "Number 5."

At the diner later, we learn that Mr. Bouchard had sold the motel last year and moved to Montreal to live with his daughter. If my father knew this, he has forgotten, and in fact, I don't think he remembers his friend at all until a slice of lemon pie arrives.

"Yves makes wonderful pastry. I should go back to thank him."

"Mr. Bouchard is not here now, Dad."

"Oh, well, we'll see him in the morning," he says, turning his attention back to his dessert.

He leaves a twenty-dollar tip because the waitress made him laugh when she brought our food, although neither she nor I knew why and exchanged gentle shrugs.

My father laughs a lot now, often at things that are not funny.

Back in Number 5, I search for something on TV, while he sits in the chair outside the door.

The sunset flames dark orange before disappearing into an inky blue sky. The air is cool and invigorating here.

"Good sleeping weather," my father says, when I check on him, adding that he might sleep in the car but he finally comes back inside.

Flipping through the channels, he stops at a cooking show in French.

We settle back on our beds, watching a wild-eyed man chop onions while declaring, "*Ils me font pleurer.*"

"What's he saying?"

"They make me cry," I tell him.

"No shit, Sherlock," he says and we laugh so hard that soon we are crying, along with the onion chopper.

I wake in the middle of the night to the cabin door open and my father outside on the chair.

"I'm waiting for that bear," he says.

Bile backs up in my throat, but I reply, "I don't think so, not tonight. Maybe tomorrow."

Smiling, he follows me back to bed.

The next morning, we sleep late and don't get moving for hours. Mr. Bouchard is forgotten.

My father offers to drive because he says I look tired, but after I

THE LIGHT IN THE SKY

assure him that I am happy to stay behind the wheel he settles back in the passenger seat.

"I wonder if we'll see any moose today? Remember last time?"

"Yes, the moose made short work of that car. The driver died, didn't he?"

"Oh, yes, he didn't have a prayer. The animal just kept on going, but I imagine it died in the woods, like that bear that passed our car."

These two incidents are only connected by our having witnessed them on the same trip.

The moose was hit by a driver ahead of us who seemed to speed up when he saw the animal, as if wanting to hit it. No one hit the bear; it simply strolled past our car, in the night, we having parked at a layby because my mother didn't want to drive any farther looking for a motel.

My father and I were the only ones to see the bear. My mother was such a heavy sleeper that she would not wake at the last trumpet, he liked to joke, until she died, and then he began worrying that she really would not wake up.

"I can't wait to go up on the cliff once more, before I die," he says, as I pull off the highway for lunch.

He has said this a dozen times since May. It is mid-August, a week before the anniversary neither of us mentions but which is on both of our minds: sixty years since two twelve-year-olds jumped off that cliff.

He has never forgiven himself for what happened, my mother told me before she died, but then patted my hand and said, "But there has been you and that soothes all."

My father is in no danger of dying anytime soon, his doctor confirmed, after giving him the all clear to make this trip.

For a man of seventy-two, he is surprisingly fit and healthy, given he never watches what he eats or exercises anymore, beyond walking (biking abandoned for now). His only real health issue is his feet, a problem since he was beaten on the soles by teachers, punishment for acting up in school. His toes are curled like claws and never really straighten. He only takes his shoes off to have a shower or at night, when he goes to bed. The shoes are always heavy, black, and impenetrable.

The sky has a strange orange cast and the smell of smoke is undeniable.

"The forest fires," I say.

"They are emptying towns northeast," the owner of the diner replies when I ask about the long line of traffic heading south.

"Precaution?"

He shrugs.

"*Merde*," he says, blushing, then, "Sorry."

"Swearing is much more elegant in French than English."

"But the same rage."

My father has returned from the bathroom.

"I used to be able to string six or eight swear words together," he says.

We all laugh at this.

"I did it once at work and one of the fellows said, 'I didn't know Newfies could be so smart'."

"They say the same about us Québécois. We are nothing. *Bâtard*."

Nodding, my father continues, "I said, 'Well, there's a few of us smart Newfies around, but I haven't encountered a smart fellow from Ontario yet.'"

The owner smiles.

We are silent for a moment, then I ask, "Are they going to close the highway?"

"Watch the phone. If yes, come back. You will stay here."

Driving on, I ask my father, "Do you remember when we stopped in Rivière-du-Loup—"

THE LIGHT IN THE SKY

"And had that wonderful spaghetti in the little restaurant."

We laugh.

"The sauce was so good. I still taste it sometimes," he says, adding, "in my mind."

"This little boy brought a basket of garlic bread, dripping with butter. Mom wouldn't have any because it was too messy."

"She was always so worried about mess and waste." My father sighs.

"You and I ate it all."

"I would have asked for more except her withering look stopped me," he says.

"She meant well."

"She always meant well."

We decide to keep driving instead of looking for another motel.

Later, he insists on visiting the Upper Town in Quebec City because, he says, my mother loved it so much, although she never did. Back on the highway hours later, the sky is inky but still with a halo of orange. The acrid-smelling smoke has gotten fainter but remains, and the line of cars heading south thinned out an hour ago. The highway now, in both directions, is eerily empty.

My father has dozed off, his snoring quiet and intermittent, but he wakes when the car slows as I pull into another of many rest stops today. I am no longer able to focus on the road and almost nodded off a few minutes before.

"We'll rest here for the night," I say.

"Yes."

There are two other vehicles under the flicking electric lights, an SUV and a truck, their occupants standing around, talking. When I park, the four adults—three children nearby are eating at a picnic table—look as my father and I get out of the car. Their faces relax when they see us, no doubt deciding we aren't a menace, and they come over to say hello.

NOT THE SAME ROAD OUT

The parents of the children, Margaret and Joe, and the younger couple from the truck, Rudy and Emily, have also decided to stay here tonight.

Like us, Margaret and Joe, along with Louie, Bobby and Katie, are heading east, to relatives in Fredericton until the fires near their farm are under control, while Rudy and Emily crossed over the median to stop here. They are on their way to Montreal, where Emily's parents live.

Later, Rudy tells us that they, too, have a farm, with two horses, which they had to set loose because they could not find anyone to transport them south.

"We're broken," he says, his eyes welling up.

"When Emily had to shoo Ginger and Theo away, she collapsed. I don't know if we will ever see them again."

My father unexpectedly folds Rudy into an embrace.

"There, there, son. You must stay strong."

We pull our vehicles close, forming a type of star so we can see each other, and exchange phone numbers.

"Not that we're expecting trouble," Joe says.

"Better safe than sorry. We are so glad you are with us," Margaret adds, while Emily nods.

The children are now piled into the back of the SUV, laughing and thinking this is a great adventure.

In front of us is a map detailing the Trans Canada Trail.

Rudy points to the Baie-Saint-Paul section and mentions that he is originally from there.

"I hope it won't be damaged by the fires this year," he says.

"No, it can't be. It's lovely, all those marshes and ponds," my father says.

"And the birds, we took the children to see the birds," Margaret says.

"My favourite is the great black-backed gull, a pirate, but what can you do?" my father says.

THE LIGHT IN THE SKY

"Louie too loves it."

My father then relates how he fell into one of the ponds and I had to fish him out.

"Katie pushed Bobbie into one."

My father leans closer to Margaret.

"I believe I was pushed, too."

She pats his arm as everyone laughs.

"Who would do such a thing to you?"

He nods my way.

"I never would, Dad."

"You have shifty eyes," Joe says and claps my father on the back.

"Don't worry, we will protect you."

Despite the hour and the stress of meeting like this, my father is happy among these strangers who seem to have quickly become friends.

"We went cross-country skiing on part of the trail, up around Charlevoix, last winter. All the huts have been renovated. The snow was like powder and the sky so blue and clear. Heaven, really," Rudy says.

"We travelled that part too, but in summer. I still have that part of the trail on my list, to travel in the winter," my father says.

He is remembering things that he hasn't spoken of for a long time, and I wonder if it is being here, among these people, that has reignited his memory and passion.

"The children want to cross-country ski around Charlevoix. We love the sport and that area has so much good food."

"Maybe we could meet up and do that some time, when our world is normal again," Emily, who hasn't spoken much, suggests.

Everyone murmurs agreement.

"That's a wonderful idea," my father says, squeezing my hand.

Before returning to our vehicles, Rudy says we should take stock of what protection we have, just to know. He and Emily have a small axe, two hammers and assorted screwdrivers from the fix-it box always in the truck.

Joe took a baseball bat before leaving the house although "Marg gave me hell for it."

"When we pulled in here, before the rest of you arrived, I said to put the bat in the front and we'd take turns beating anyone who tried to hurt our kids."

There is an undercurrent of anxiety weaving through the laughter now.

"Too many scary movies," Joe says.

When it is our turn to declare, my father looks at me.

"Two folding, Japanese knives with blades like lances. I could cut your throat from ear to ear in one attempt."

"Well, maybe I could bunk in with one of you, seeing that disturbing gleam in my daughter's eyes," my father says and more laughter erupts.

"Of course, we're more likely to encounter four-legged animals instead of two, tonight, especially moose and bears. They've been heading south, too," Rudy says.

I imagine he is hoping that Ginger and Theo are, as well.

Later, my father notices filings of rusted metal around a garbage can by the washroom. The rust reminds him of the iron ore dust on the island.

"It coated everything. The girls made a paste of it to smear on the dark circles under their eyes," he says, before heading inside.

I wait for him at the entrance because I am afraid that he will get disoriented at this late hour and in this strange place and wander into the woods if left alone.

"You're in the men's washroom, Elizabeth," he says, when he walks out of the stall.

"It's only you and me."

He smiles through the mirror as he washes his hands.

"You think I'll run off."

"No, I—"

"There's no cliff here to run to."

"Dad, please."

The night air is warm but I shudder as we walk back to the car, until he puts his arm around me and draws me close.

He crawls into the back seat and stretches out, but it is not long before Rudy knocks at the window and hands me a plastic bag with granola bars, apples and a softening banana.

"Emily said to ask if you have water?"

"We do, yes. Thanks for this."

From the back, my father stretches a long arm towards Rudy, opening his hand to reveal two chocolate bars and a bag of cashews.

"Thanks, Tom. We love cashews but don't get them often. Too expensive."

"Well, there will be more in the morning, for breakfast," my father says, grinning.

We sleep for a bit after that, until I wake to patting on my shoulder.

"A lot of people on the island got cancer," he begins. "I think it was the iron ore dust. When we sneezed, it came out of our noses, when we spit, we spit orange."

"I didn't know that."

"Your mother died because of that place. I will, too."

He is quiet for a moment before saying, "Your grandfather and great uncles killed the ones who hurt us boys, you know that, don't you?"

His eyes are watering now.

"I suspected so, but you never said. Why are you telling me now, Dad?"

"It's important that you know things, before it's too late."

"All right."

"It was so black that night, not a light in the sky, as if God was giving them cover to do what they had to. My mother buttoned my father into his old jacket and said, 'We won't speak of it again, boys,' before kissing him and his brothers and opening the back door. I thought I was out of sight in the hall."

"Grandmother was like Mom?"

"Yes, the eyes of an eagle. Nothing escaped her. The police ignored what happened, and the Roman Catholic Church, well, we've learned about them and their antics, over the years."

I am kneeling now on the front seat.

His hands are working his thin fingers as if trying to make them longer.

"No one ever found them, but the North Atlantic is deep and those three were well weighed down. Their wives didn't even make much fuss."

"They weren't priests?"

"No, laymen, who ran the summer camp. I wasn't supposed to be there, as an Anglican, but I wanted to go camping with my friends, and the priest said yes, if my father agreed. He never forgave himself for letting me go. My mother threatened the wrath of God on the lot of them, but they shooed her away, like another nuisance female. I think it was her who gave my father permission. He wouldn't have done what he did, I don't think, if she hadn't."

"Why did John and Donnie still jump off the cliff, after those men were killed?"

"I didn't think they would go through with the plan after the men disappeared, but Donnie said the priest was already calling for him at midnight and sooner or later his mother would give in and send him along, to keep peace in the house. What happened to him was never going to happen again, he said, and John agreed."

"It wasn't your fault, Dad."

"We were the Three Musketeers, one for all and all for one, but on that night, at that crucial moment, I didn't try to stop them. I didn't say anything, as first Donnie and then John stepped off into the air and landed on the rocks below."

"It's okay."

"No, I was mad with them. I thought their jumping made my father and uncles' actions, their courage all for nothing, but more than that, I suddenly got afraid that there was nothing after this life and that my best friends would be shunted off into unconsecrated ground and forgotten."

"You didn't forget them."

"I'm forgetting them now, like I'm forgetting your mother and you, just a bit at a time, the way my mother forgot."

The wind has picked up, blowing dust around the car in little cyclones. I see Rudy asleep, while Emily looks out the window, probably thinking about her horses.

"It's a brutal thing, forgetting," my father says.

"There are good treatments now for dementia and Alzheimer's. We will talk with your doctor when we get back."

"Yes?"

"And you can afford the drugs, since you're as rich—"

"—as Rockefeller."

The laughter is like balm, soothing us.

"Will you be with me, even after I forget you?"

"Until the last trumpet, Dad."

He reaches for my hand, stroking it, starting to say something else but I put a finger to my lips and point out the window, in time for him to see the bear look at us as it passes the car. It doesn't stop and soon disappears into the woods.

"Good thing I didn't run away," he says.

"Yes, good thing."

"It's not as big as the other one."

"But big enough," I say, and text our nighttime companions to alert them. *We are not alone.*

NOT THE SAME ROAD OUT

"Can you imagine this happening again, Dad?"

"Yes, I can still imagine," he says, before folding himself back onto the seat, smiling as he drifts off to sleep.

Emily texts: *Saw it, thanks. Your father would enjoy the trail in winter?*

He would love it. It's one of the last trips on his list.

We will be in touch.

I look out the window to Emily waving goodnight. She looks so vulnerable, reminding me of my father now, with his legs drawn up to his chest and his hands clasped under his chin.

After taking a photograph of him, I turn the radio on low, almost hoping Reverend Jim will be there, reciting First Corinthians but it is a DJ in Montreal, saying the fires are coming under control.

"That's a bit of a Hallelujah for us all," he says, then adds, "And here's one of the best covers of Leonard Cohen's 'Hallelujah,' by Jeff Buckley, an American singer who died more than twenty years ago. He was only thirty but left us with this blessing."

My father sighs in his sleep as I settle back to melodic guitar cords.

The sky begins to lighten around the edges of the blackness.

"Hallelujah," Buckley sings, as soft as a whisper.

Yes, Hallelujah.

Soldiers Summit

MATTHEW HENEGHAN

Yukon | Dempster Highway

At the edge of the world there exists a special kind of silence. It's not the kind of quiet you get in a library or the awkward obligatory hush of an elevator ride. This is the kind of silence that makes you hear your own heartbeat as if it were a drum being played within you, the soft crush of your boots against dirt, and the nagging little voice in your head that won't let you forget all the things you're trying to leave behind. A suffocating silence that refuses a tired soul respite. The kind of silence that swallows you whole. Consumes you.

That's what I was walking into when I took the trail up Goldensides, a mountain in the Ogilvies. A place as rugged as it is beautiful. Isolated, just stone and sky, a rutted land that boasts a quiet, austere beauty without ego.

It was a promise that got me here. A promise made over a decade ago in a hot, dusty wadi halfway across the world.

"Swear to me, Aiden," Colin said, leaning back in the shade of a tattered tarp, a half-smoked cigar dangling from his fingers. "When this is all over, you'll come to the Yukon. We'll hit the Dempster and hike Goldensides." His smile broke into a chuckle. "Ya gotta laugh . . ."

"What?"

"The place I love so much is in Tombstone National Park—a name like that seems more befitting to where we are now, not there.

NOT THE SAME ROAD OUT

Not home." He chortled again. "But believe me, it's the closest thing you'll see to heaven on Earth. If I can't get there with ya and show it to you, do me a favour and go see it for yourself, brother. It's worth it." He reached into his pocket and shoved a crumpled photo into my hand like it was a lifeline; him standing on the edge of some ridgeline, clouds draped low over the valley below. "Someday," he said, tapping the image, "you'll see it. No excuses. You hear me?"

What else could I do? I promised. I never knew why it was so important to him. Neither of us could have suspected why it would become so important to me either.

Back then, we were just soldiers pretending to be invincible, or believing we were, laughing in the face of death with cigars we could barely afford and whisky we definitely couldn't, making plans for the future. Colin had this way of seeing the world like it was his own private joke. The punchline finally caught up to him on a street in Kandahar. Though nothing was particularly charming or funny that day.

He died there. I didn't. Not physically, anyway.

I'm not here to unpack the guilt that comes with that kind of imbalance—you couldn't fit that into a backpack if you tried. It wasn't that I didn't want to come here, to this place—I'd thought about it all the time. But life has a way of getting away from you. At first, it was the little things. Like starting a new job as a paramedic in Cold Lake after deployment—different uniform, different ghosts, same tired road of life's failed endeavours. I chose it because it was familiar, because routine, even if macabre, felt like the only raft on an otherwise rudderless sea. But the calls were different now. Everything was. I'd freeze behind the wheel sometimes, headlights glaring back at me like accusation. After one call, I sat in the rig outside Tim Horton's for forty minutes, pretending to finish paperwork, just so I didn't have to go home to silence.

Then came bigger things. There was Lois. She wore a satin

off-white dress with small sunflowers embroidered on the bodice on our wedding day, even though the weatherman promised rain. Said she wanted to bring her own sunlight. We got married in a tiny hall in Bonnyville. For a while, we made it work. We built a life out of humble routines: her morning tea, my night shifts, the way she'd leave the porch light on even when I didn't make it home.

But grief has a way of fermenting and eventually it turns to poison. I stopped talking and she stopped asking. One morning she found me asleep on the bathroom floor spooning with an empty bottle—again—and just stood there, defeated and dejected, staring like she didn't recognize the man she'd said yes to. That was the beginning of the end. Paperwork followed. Resentful silences replaced laughter and kindness. A house that echoed with everything we weren't saying.

After that, the nights got longer. I spent too many of them at a place called the Rusty Lantern, this half-forgotten tavern off 50th Street. I liked the corner booth by the busted jukebox because no one ever asked questions there. I drank with men whose names I never learned. Sometimes we'd talk about sports, sometimes about nothing. Most of the time, I just listened—to the clink of glass, the low hum of neon, and the static of a life I no longer recognized.

If I'm honest, I think I was scared. Scared of what I'd feel—of standing here without him and facing the weight of what I lost. It's been sixteen years. Sixteen. And somehow, even with all that time gone by, it still feels like yesterday . . . and a thousand lifetimes ago. But on my last birthday, it hit me: Colin never got to be in his forties. He never made it out of his twenties. The world kept turning, but he stayed exactly the same in my mind—forever young, frozen in that uniform, in that smile.

If I didn't come now, I might never come at all. And he'd never forgive me.

Oh, who the hell am I kidding?

Yes, he would.

It's me that wouldn't forgive myself.

A promise is a promise, and Colin had made me swear. He was from Dawson City, born and raised, and he talked about the Yukon like someone talks about an old flame—wistful, aching, like something beautiful that slipped away in the night without a note or a goodbye.

He said he'd spent a lot of time hiking those mountains as a teenager, meandering through the brush with no real destination—just the sound of wind and footfall, the occasional eagle cry overhead. "It's a mute button," he said once, "for the world." I didn't understand what he meant until much later.

Now, I'm here, just like I promised. Forty-two-years old and two full steps into a midlife crisis, trudging up the trail with a head full of memories that felt heavier than the pack on my back.

The trail was a bastard. A real son of a bitch. Perhaps not from a younger perspective—but from mine it was damn n ear Sisyphean.

It started off simple enough, a soft incline winding through uneven ground. In the shade it smelled like Labrador Tea, faintly spicy, earthy. The air held that crisp, clean taste that doesn't exist anywhere else. But the higher I climbed, the steeper it got, and pretty soon my legs were screaming louder than my brain. It's funny, being in your forties, somehow your mind still believes you to be in your twenties, and only in moments like the one I was in are we shown the true nature of that fallacy.

There's something about physical pain that clears the cobwebs in your head. With every step, I felt a little less like the broken-down ex-soldier trying to hold it together back in the real world and a little more like just another guy putting one foot in front of the other. Left, right, left . . . ironic, really. You can leave the army with a heart and mind as broken as the body, and yet the only way to heal is to keep moving forward. Or, in my very specific case, up.

SOLDIERS SUMMIT

Then the memories hit, like an unexpected storm.

It was stupid stuff at first—Colin laughing so hard he spit coffee all over me, or the way he used to hum Sinatra songs under his breath when he was stressed. Little things that made him human, not just the cardboard cutout they put on his memorial card. His laugh—as contagious as it was potent. I could almost hear it playing on the breeze that danced across the juniper.

Then, as always, came the heavier stuff.

The explosion. The smell of burnt rubber and blood fornicating together in some sick embrace. The way Colin's body looked so small under that black tarp. People don't tell you about that part when they talk about being a soldier. The way death makes everything small. The way nothing ever looks the same afterward. When I first got back, I'd sometimes see his face on strangers in supermarkets, sidewalks, movie theatres. I felt like a crazy person for a lot of years. When Lois and I got married, there was an empty seat at the head table. For the man who'd never show up or give a best-man speech. A man who couldn't. When I got divorced, I'd sit next to an empty barstool in the Rusty Lantern and croon my sorrow to the ghost that sat in it. Even though Colin wasn't around, he was with me everywhere I went.

I stopped for a break halfway up the ridge, sitting on a rock that jutted out like a throne for weary hikers. Or maybe nature was just telling me to slow down, knowing I was pushing too hard. I pulled out the old careworn photo Colin had gifted me back in Afghanistan and turned it over in my hands. It was faded and torn at the edges, a far cry from the pristine copy his parents probably kept back home in Dawson City. But this was the part he wanted me to have, the part he said belonged here, where the sky touched the earth. Where problems faded on the wind and souls weighed less than they do in any city.

"Almost there, buddy," I muttered, as if he could hear me. I often spoke just above a whisper to Colin. It helped combat all those quiet moments I faced without him.

The final stretch was brutal. Like walking on a treadmill going nowhere.

The trail narrowed to little more than a goat path, with jagged rocks on one side and a drop that would make even the most fearless adrenalin junkie twinge. My legs felt like they were made of lead, and every breath came with a side of fire and a wheeze that mimicked death.

But then I reached it. The summit. The goddamned top of the world. Colin always said it was a view worth seeing before you cash out, and he wasn't wrong. He rarely was.

The valley spread out below me in a patchwork of greens and varying browns, with clusters of dwarf willows and Arctic cotton grass. The Yukon River meandered in the distance, silver against the endless expanse of tundra. Indolent mountains rose and crawled in the distance; their peaks capped with snow that glowed in the late afternoon sun. It was the kind of view that makes you believe in God, even if you stopped going to church years ago.

I stood there for a while, absorbing all of it. The wind whipped around me and for the first time in a long time, I felt . . . quiet. Not the kind of quiet you get in the absence of noise, but the kind that comes when you finally quell all the voices in your head. The echoes of regret and melancholy.

I took out the photograph and sat on the edge of the ridge, legs dangling.

"All right, brother," I said, my voice barely making a sound. "This is it. Your heaven on Earth. Welcome home."

I held the photo in my hands one last time before letting it catch the current of a passing wind, or maybe an angel's graceful hand. For a moment, it was like watching a part of him become the air, the land, the sky. In that final act of releasing my last tangible link to Colin, he somehow felt more alive to me than I'd ever thought possible.

I don't know if he was there with me in some cosmic, spectral sense, but I felt him in that moment. Felt the weight of his absence and the strange comfort of keeping my promise. I could almost hear his voice. I wanted to speak to it. To have it respond, but I didn't. I just shut myself up and listened to my friend talk in the silence.

I stayed on the ridge until the sun started to move toward the horizon, washing the sky in shades of marigold and violet.

There's a cliché about closure that people love to throw around, like grief is some kind of door you can slam shut and lock forever. Grief isn't a door. It's a ghost. A thing you can't see but always feel. It sits at your table, follows you down grocery store aisles, whispers to you in the quiet moments.

For years, I'd saved his home number in my phone, like somehow deleting it would be the real goodbye. Every time something funny or messed up happened, my first instinct was still to call him. On road trips, I'd catch myself looking out at some stretch of highway and think, Colin would've loved this view, like he was just behind me in the backseat, waiting to weigh in with some sarcastic remark. When I bought my first house, I caught myself thinking about where he'd crash—air mattress or couch?—before remembering he'd never see it. And some nights I'd unfold that picture he left me. I could barely look at it. I'd just hold it in my hands as if it were about to disappear.

As I made my way back down the trail, the silence followed me, but it wasn't the same as before. It wasn't the kind that reminded me of everything I'd lost. It was the kind that reminded me I was still here, still breathing, still putting one foot in front of the other.

The way down felt simpler. It wasn't. Not mechanically, or anything. But I'll say this for emotional weight: it weighs far more than anything you need for a day's hike.

I stopped at the rock formation that jutted out into a makeshift bench and sat down again, giving my burning old legs a brief reprieve from the trail. It was almost entirely dark now. A canopy of glitter had opened itself above me, bedazzling the sky in a brilliant flicker of dots and infinity. All the woes of my world fell into that expansive sea of limitless sparkle. Was Colin at rest there? Had he seen what I had done? That I had finally fulfilled my promise, even all these years later?

I knew in that moment, sitting on stone, that there would never come a day in which I would not grieve the loss of my friend. Coming here to his most beloved place did bring a sense of closure that I had been hiding from for a lot of years. But it also solidified the finality of his absence. I had nothing physical left of his to hold onto. The photo now only a memory, nothing more. I turned on my headlamp and began walking again.

Somehow, for whatever reason—be it the scenery, the day's undertaking, or the entirety of the landscape itself—I faced myself. What had my life in the last sixteen years been? Little more than a chaotic series of self-destructive acts. I knew that I wasn't living as the man who Colin had befriended should be. He would have been ashamed of me. I was ashamed of me.

Vegetation of some kind brushed against my legs, and a shift occurred within me. A realignment of sorts. In accepting that grief would always be with me, I began to see what life, and the living of it, could grant me. And I began to understand my responsibility—not just to Colin and the others who sacrificed so much—but also to myself and those who love me. I could change. Make amends.

On my way down, when checking the route on the map, I noticed that one of the places I'd been navigating was called Soldiers Summit. I laughed. And I remembered Colin's chortle.

When I got back to the car, parked at the side of the Dempster, I plopped my stuff into the hatchback, and sat in the driver's seat. I just sat there for a while, allowing the hum of nothingness to serenade me. I don't know when I started the car and began driving. It was late into the evening when I made it to the junction where the Dempster meets Hwy 2. I pulled onto the shoulder for a few hours of shut-eye.

In the morning, a rabble of birds acted as my alarm. I couldn't see them, but I heard their playful chorus.

I noticed a few bars of reception on my phone now and scrolled through my contacts. Then I pressed the button to phone her.

Colin's mother.

The phone rang a couple of times, almost granting me the chance to chicken out. But my hands refused.

"Hello."

"Hey. Kathy? This is Aiden. How are ya?"

"Oh, Aiden—good. Good. How are you? What are you up to?"

"Me? I—uh—I'm . . . I'm just . . ."

"Aiden?"

"Yeah. Sorry." I began to choke up a bit, making it hard to finish what I want to say.

"Aiden, are you here? Did you head up to the mountains? To Tombstone?"

She knew.

"Yes. Yes, I am."

"He'd be proud of you. You know that?"

"Hey, listen. I wanted to say something to you. Something I think I wanted to say years ago but never knew how." I paused.

"Okay . . ."

"I want to say thank you. Thank you for raising a good boy. Thank you for lending him to the world and making it a better place for a while. But . . . mostly . . . I guess . . . Thank you for having patience with me. I know I'm not easy."

"Oh, Aiden. Nothing about the life you chose and the loss of Colin is easy, my dear. Life isn't supposed to be easy."

"It's not? Why the hell not?" I said through a forced chuckle.

"Come see us. How far away are you? I'll make you a big Dawson breakfast and tell you why not."

"You know what, Kathy? That actually sounds nice. I'm just at the highway junction with the Dempster—gimme forty minutes or so and I'll be there."

Static

DEE HOBSBAWN-SMITH

Saskatchewan | Wakamow Valley Trail

After Paolo Uccello's *The Hunt in the Forest* (1470)

The concierge said, "You a runner? Yes, a good trail not far from here. Just past the train tracks, runs a fair ways out in the valley south of town. Easy to find. That Wakamow Valley Trail."

As she said thanks, she sensed his undertone—*My coffee's gone cold, get going you batshit old lady, God knows who you think you are going running, but I need to take a leak, so get off my patch.* She glanced back at him, saw that he knew she'd tuned him in, the lines around his cheeks and nose tightening in a sneer.

The doorman pointed down the street. "Turn left, right at the gas station, then under the train tracks. You can't miss it." His smile a little twinkle of dimples. "And you be safe out there in my people's valley, little sister."

But be wary—she caught his thought. A kind one. But saying she couldn't miss it. There was a red flag—that what she sought was easily missed. But along with the wariness, a hint of excitement crept in. Where something could be missed also existed the possibility of the unexpected.

It had been the unexpected that had made her life interesting. Whether or not "interesting" equated to "better" was for the jury to decide, and it was still out. But "unexpected" had meant children, who had learned to shield some of their feelings from her as they became adults—*Mom, I got this, it's okay*—and life raising children had been a master class in dealing with the unexpected.

As she bent and tightened her laces, the television monitor on the wall showed a split-screen shot of the American president and Canadian prime minister as they explained the most recent wrinkle in the ongoing trade war. A nightmare, she thought for the hundredth time, and began to warm up as she walked toward the valley.

Half past six on a spring morning, as a red sun rose through the haze here at fifty degrees north latitude, she remembered Jasper National Park burning almost a year ago, hundreds of kilometres west and north. Smoke had filtered south for weeks, as frightening and insidious as bad news from south of the border. But the morning was clear, despite the early-scarlet sunlight, so she headed south under the train overpass and set out toward the waiting river valley asleep beneath the early light. As she approached, she understood why this sheltered piece of land had been sacred, a gathering place for Indigenous peoples for ten thousand years. She began to run, easing into the lulling rhythm of motion. That sense of the sacred— it was part of why she ran. Why she sought out quiet rural spaces to run in, to be present in. To reach that inner part of herself, the part that had retreated through the years in self-protection—the core of her self that felt and saw and breathed and smelled and touched and heard, all with the same unified sense of healing and wholeness with the world. Being in the valley, even just for the one morning, walking or running the paths, could be nothing but good for her soul as well as her body. Crucial, really.

In the early 1900s, the train had been crucial to the town of Moose Jaw—Al Capone, Prohibition, prostitution, booze, River Road, escape tunnels. Not all of it true. Or was it? Who could tell what was true anymore? At this moment, all she read was a jamming of the forcefield, a shouting static that pounded and blurred her perceptions. Early morning silence carried its own music that interfered with her other senses.

In truth, she considered herself a deer. Not a mule deer, not a whitetail, but an amalgam of both, with a flag of a tail and high-flapping ears, elongated whitetail's body with a mule deer's spring-coiled legs and tightly-wound core suspension that sent her bouncing and bounding over fences and gates and into stands of aspens like a pogo stick. She saw herself as still She, but double-gendered, both doe and buck, gifted with invisible, late-evolving filigreed horns at her forehead that weren't bulky at all but branch-like at their essence, fine filaments of nerve strung through shimmering silver webs, an electromagnetic field that in her most recent decade had allowed her to pick up other creatures' thoughts.

She thought back to Capone. The city's present-day lustre relied heavily on spinning his grimy booze business of an earlier era, just as modern politicians spun the truth at will into something unrecognizable. She remembered the warm voice of Peter Gzowski back in the day. She'd been a fan for most of his fifteen-year tenure, listening with regret when his last gig on *Morningside* was recorded live on CBC Radio in 1997 at Temple Gardens Spa, the same hotel she'd been sleeping at these past few nights, lapping up its slightly faded luxury. Back then, Connie Kaldor sang farewell to the National Conversation, to Gzowski thinking out loud in company five days a week, three hours a day every morning, her piano keys in the background. The show, he'd said, made him, "Think fast but speak slowly"—and reflected on the air "what we can't cut, what's essential to being Canadian."

Kilometre one. The sign read Lorne Calvert Campground, a shaky image of the bridge echoing in the sleepy river, the entire scene wrapped in a suggestion of mist.

Who was she anymore? She barely knew. A widow, still a mother but not needed—the pinch and ache that wouldn't end when she'd realized that she needed her kids more than they needed her anymore. Nearing the end-decades of her creative output as a faïence artist, although she was currently working on some cutwork plates, similar to Portuguese lace-motif woven clay baskets, but rooted in the history of antique Hutterite plates dating back to the 1600s. Overtly brilliant saturated colours, especially the achingly intense turquoise-green derived from copper, still made her heart ache with *duende*, that mystical Spanish spark that connects the maker with everything. She was still an elder—at this age, there was no going back to youth. Still a woman, no doubt about it, but without the appetites that had defined her for so many years—that voracious love of sex and fabric and food and their many textures and flavours, the tensility of clay before firing so like the slickness of wet skin, the sheer stunning beauty of a translucent glaze alight with the sun, so close to the varying and living shades of sky and ocean.

She turned right and entered the silent campground, looped up and down several spacious laneways, studying the collection of early-season visitors' trailers, campers, and motorhomes, a proud row of black-and-silver Harley Davidson motorcycles aligned beside a mismatched row of tents, remnants of last night's drinks and campfires, stacks of wood for tonight's. As she came level with the last trailer, still pinned to a dusty Ford pickup, the trailer door opened and a lean man in denim climbed out, stepping almost into her path, the cigarette in his mouth already smouldering.

Unexpected. She veered sharply away, turning her head to look closely at him, passing just a few feet away, memorizing his shape. *Just in case.* He met her eyes calmly, his lips pursing around his smoke. He could have reached out and grabbed her shoulder if he'd wanted. A few decades ago, she'd have speeded up and fled, close to panic at the possibilities of what might happen, but she was older now, and calmer, and had learned that some things can't be negotiated away, and others can't be fled from, no matter how fleet the feet. As she moved down the lane she looked back, lifted one arm, waved, saw him nod, heard his voice. "Good morning." And beneath it—*Lookin' strong, you go girl, keep runnin'.*

The static in her head abruptly stopped two kilometres later, when she came to a halt at the sight of a whitetail doe motionless on the narrow trail, tail down, ears flicking, flash-frozen—*Cousin*—silent greeting between them. The doe casually dropped her head and cropped the early-spring grass as the woman slowly resumed running, then passed the doe, still grazing. Who did she trust that deeply? Let in that closely? She pondered—two children, sister, three best friends—was that all?—as she swung effortlessly around the next curve and the doe disappeared from sight.

She turned onto the Devonian Trail, past the sign reading Wakamow Valley Authority. Passed a concrete turtle and laughed. Double irony. On impulse, she doubled back to the turtle. Its raised face smiling at her, its painted orange eyes gleaming—*Sister! You have been so long! Welcome!* The tiles lining its back were cool under her hand as she buffed them back to brilliance—a rainbow of turquoise, teal, aquamarine, burnt sienna, sunny yellow, fuchsia. Fumbling in the grass, she pulled up a handful of fresh green and tucked it into the turtle's mouth.

Kilometre five. Her feet pounded a tattoo. Somehow she'd picked up the pace, caught in her surroundings instead of monitoring her watch. It felt like she was being pursued: her breathing was elevated, her cadence close to max, her heart rate redlining out of zone four's threshold into zone five, adrenalin coursing through her bloodstream like a greyhound on the scent. But who was hounding her? Or what? If this were a quest, she thought, then she was the hart and the hind, the objects of the hunt. The hunted. But why was she feeling like the pursued and not the pursuer? Hadn't she been the one chasing success—chasing happiness, that elusive flying mystery—all her life?

NOT THE SAME ROAD OUT

Her stride lengthened and her pace eased. This velocity was great for short pipe-openers and time trials but wasn't sustainable for today's long run. As her tempo eased, she counted *one two three four* repeatedly, slowing the cadence until she needed no glance at her Garmin to tell her that her heart rate was throttling back as well. A few hundred metres later, she settled into her unhurried eat-the-kilometres lope and stable heart rate, and the scenery came back into focus.

Kilometre seven. In River Park, she came to an arbour covered in weathered vines, leaves just taking shape, their story unreadable. Stopping briefly to scrutinize the nascent tangle, she wondered what they could say about cross-border rumrunners and loose morals along River Road. About presidents who treated lying like a day's sport, who viewed trade agreements as mere scraps of paper and borders as artificially drawn lines.

A trade war. That's what tariffs are. The former PM, Justin Trudeau, Trudeau the Younger, had said, "It might mean opting for Canadian rye over Kentucky bourbon . . . we prefer to solve our disputes with diplomacy but we're ready to fight when necessary."

She'd lost her taste for booze, even wine, so that part of the high tensions between her country and its neighbour to the south no longer impinged on her pocketbook. But like all her neighbours, friends, and family, she too felt her nationalism more strongly than ever these days. What other greed did this trade war conceal? She'd feared Trump's lunacy in his first term, and his second term's unleashed mania for Canada, Greenland, and Ukraine seemed to her to indicate greed for her home and native land, all of it, its natural resources, minerals, water, ice, seashores, mountains. She'd taken to sending emails to the new prime minister's office, offering words of support, admonition, encouragement, and no fault or blame. The world was already too toxic. She'd always hoped that her pottery, with those brilliant glazes, helped to dissipate the hatred.

STATIC

Maybe she should send the PM a pair of the new plates after they emerged from the kiln.

Kilometre eight. A suspension bridge, wooden slats and rope handles swaying beneath her running feet, chicken wire the only shelter from falling. The static in her head increased. She heard again the buzz of her parents' old Philips radio as they tuned in to the prime minister, Trudeau the Elder, speaking in Washington in 1969: "Living next to you is in some ways like sleeping with an elephant."

When she tripped, the bridge pitched like a bronc and she rolled several times, caught and cradled, held safely by the wire, the wood, the sun, the sky.

The watch on her wrist vibrated. *Fall Detected. A message has been sent to your emergency contacts.* Her dead husband, her sole contact, the list not updated in the year since his death. As she lay motionless, her inner core felt like a sheet of glazed ceramic, something fragile and tenuous that suddenly crackled like a glaze that crazed as it shrank in the kiln. *Be still, be still, be still.*

Lying flat on her back on the bridge, the sky seemed enormous, even more enormous than a prairie sky normally seemed. The sun had burned through its early-morning amber and scarlet, and hung in full majesty of gold in a sky of Prussian blue fading to lapis lazuli edges. She breathed gingerly, testing her lungs, her arms, her ribcage. Nothing seemed damaged, so she lay back and let go a long breath of relief. *Thank you.*

She was unprepared for the response. *Of course. We've got you, little sister. Come, let's mend you again. Pick up the pieces and go home.*

Heart shaking, when she held the crackled shards of her life edge to mismatched edge, she saw a disjointed pair of eyes, a mismatched pair of ears: Them, converging into Her/She/Us, looking back at her, the face in the mirroring glaze and her own united again, whole at last, but recast in a strange new form, knit together with seams and welts and scars. She looked closely at each scar, each piece of damage, each bit of broken heart and torn tenderness, wondering how they had welded themselves together. Into oneness.

And it came to her that the *how* didn't matter. What did matter was that she *had* loved, still loved, was loved in return. She had children, friends, a sister, all of whom loved her. She *had* mended. She had lived, and broken, and lived on, still broken, until her broken bits had healed, whole again, never as she had been, but whole, and made utilitarian—made useful still, if no longer beautiful—by mending.

She got to her feet and brushed off her knees. Not much blood. She'd be fine. Just three kilometres to go.

The Boat

PATRICK WOODCOCK

Nunavut | Frobisher Bay

PROLOGUE

Sometimes I imagined the whole world as a cylinder spinning inside a music box. What song would resonate from Iqaluit's ridges? Would its melody rise in a triumphant major key, celebrating those who endured the dissonance of cold and colonialism? Or would it unfold in a mournful minor chord, a pianissimo lament for the ones diminished by the weight of others' beliefs.

I've never heard music—not the way others describe it—but I've felt what it does. When people around me sing or even just think about singing, something changes. Even the ones I can't stand seem . . . softer.

Once, I came across another boat, drifting in from somewhere else. When we collided, its words made no sense to me. But its cry—how it pierced to the root. Pain and boredom sound the same, no matter where you're from. The language may shift, but the tone of sorrow is universal.

I learned once from a doctor leaving Iqaluit—he wanted to see the land from the sea—that when people are sad, their amygdala lights up, flooded with emotion. The prefrontal cortex dims, making choices harder, clouding judgment. Serotonin, dopamine, norepinephrine—all of them falter, pulling mood and energy down like an anchor in deep water.

NOT THE SAME ROAD OUT

It was interesting, but like Business English, I found Medical English uninspiring. I didn't need the science. I only needed to know they were hurting. And I did what I could, held my old hull together so that maybe, just maybe, the sway of open water could soothe them.

We are all shaped by what and how we touch, aren't we? A hug feels different than lifting a chair. The Arctic hugs differently than most places, it is a shifting, fluid, beautiful, and sometimes fatal embrace that must be respected.

I must tell you—trees are far wiser than you think. It may ache to hear this, to realize what knowledge was silenced when our elders were felled. A tree learns by resonance—through living touch. Only when something alive brushes against its bark does the song begin, a quiet transcription of memory passed from host to trunk, note by note, breath by branch.

And yes, we can speak back. Even when we're cut and reshaped into something else, our knowledge does not fade. It lingers in the grain, in the memory of what we were, if you're willing to listen. But that's the thing: no adults hear us anymore. Perhaps once, long ago, when human lives moved in smaller circles and hearts beat in open time, they could. But now, as they age, they drift out of tune. Numbed, wrapped in their own static, muffled behind the walls they build to keep out the world's discord, only to be drowned in it.

But when a child clambered up one of my branches, we spoke for hours in a quiet duet. The youngest don't say much—just laughter, bright and untamed, like wind riffing through leaves. But I feel their joy, raw and resonant. As they grow, the melody changes. They begin to speak in softer tones, guarding our harmonies like a treasured refrain. They know what adults would say. So, they fall silent—not from disbelief, but from a tremolo of fear. Fear of being dismissed, misheard, muted.

THE BOAT

And then they leave. All of them do. There is so much in the world to see, to chase, to become.

Yet I have learned from them—those who once climbed me, and those who now climb into what I've become, laying their hands on my gunwale in storm-tossed hours. I've learned of art, of history, of politics and love—carried on voices that rode the salt wind like a chorus echoing through time. But I've also felt the ache of war, the stillness of death, the heat of disease. The weight of betrayal and loss—etched like a sorrowful refrain into the trembling fingers of the grieving, the searching, the ones who arrived with more questions than answers.

Some journeys across Frobisher Bay were joy itself—sky alight, laughter spilling over the water. Others I wish had never happened. It is strange, how the same hands can carry both wisdom and cruelty. How the same touch can hold genius and such staggering folly.

WAITING

Today will be discordant—I felt it in the hands of my captain: the tension, the reluctance, like a bow drawn too tight. Four men are coming for their final passage. It's their third day on me, and already they've become a quartet of the most self-absorbed souls I've ever borne.

To hear their inner monologues, you might think they've suffered. But I know better. Whatever bruises they carry are surface-level, mere grace notes compared to the deeper tragedies that play out here, season after season, in quieter keys. Like most from the south, they come not to listen, not to learn the stories, the beauty, the bounty. They come to extract—leaving with their pockets heavier, their egos more inflated, blind to the harm their presence scores into this place.

Though I am not religious, I prayed the weather would shift. I wished for wind, for swell—for any unrest that might ground me. But the tide returns now, lifting me from the soft cradle of muck where some of my dearest companions dwell. Everything alive gives something. But the wind is still. My body barely stirs. The day, it seems, will play on.

Soon we'll head out again, toward the place where the flow edge might have been, had the bay still worn its winter skin. If only the temperature would fall—sharp enough to force gloves onto their hands—then perhaps I'd be spared their touch.

I hate to sound so bitter. But if ever there was a day to let the fracture in my hull widen—to keep us moored or carry us just far enough that their voices dissolve into the ocean's unresolved chord—this would be it. For now, I must endure them a little longer. Just a few more measures of this unwelcome song.

I feel sorry for my captain. He's worn thin by worry—about his family, his finances, and now, more and more, whether this will be the year I finally give up on him.

Truthfully, it is harder than it once was. My joints groan with the weight of years. But I remember the day I was first cut down—the confusion, the severance. The workers wore gloves; I felt nothing. I didn't know what was happening to me, only that everything familiar had ended.

It wasn't until the master shipbuilder laid his bare hands on me—warm, steady, deliberate—that I understood. I was being remade. Not destroyed but shaped into something with rhythm and reach. A vessel to carry lives across the bay, to thread together communities to the north and south. Yes, they had shortened my time in the forest. But they gave that time purpose. A kind one, I believed then. I would be an instrument of care, of labour, of movement.

I wish I could say the same for everyone who boards me. Some bring such tightly coiled shame, such dense, private darkness that I feel it pressing into my frame like creeping rot. And I'll admit—there are moments I've wished they'd drink just a little more, lean too far over the gunwale, and vanish into the welcoming waves.

THE BOAT

But still, I remain—for my captain, whom I respect, and for the hundreds of companions I've carried through the years. Some adults bring their children, and we share a symphony of laughter, bright and unguarded.

I nod traded greetings with belugas who pass beneath me, slipping through the water like whispered notes, pausing just long enough to sense whether I carry hunters. If not, more arrive—playful, curious—dancing beneath the sightseers' awe like light through the shallows.

I love the touch of seals. They press their whole bodies to my hull before launching away, a soft percussion of life. Through them, I've learned of distant communities—smaller, wilder, more fragile—with melodic names like Arctic Bay and Pond Inlet, each one echoing like a refrain across the northern sea.

Only once did I have the privilege of speaking with a bowhead whale. He had heard of me and approached while those aboard were lost in their lenses. With the care of a master carver, he touched his great jaw to my keel. We exchanged stories—brief, hushed, careful. He could not linger long, not with the eyes above, searching.

I met a narwhal too. Its language was harder to decipher—more distant, more internal—but I understood enough. It was lost. I told it to rest beneath me awhile. When its smooth, blubbery skin brushed mine, I felt the weight of forty years: migrations traced through shifting currents, calves raised and mourned. Yet there was no bitterness in its voice. Even those who had taken its young were not blamed—had it not consumed Arctic cod to survive?

Years later, a carver sat aboard, speaking softly of a family tale he had etched into the spiralling tusk of a narwhal. I thought: what a tender way for them both to live on—not in sadness, but in story.

Damn, here they come.

I can feel the thud of their coolers—weighted with booze—pressing down against my deck like a warning drum. Each time a hand grazes my rails as they clamber aboard, I catch a dissonant chord of their mood. Four of them. Four puzzled men with equally muddled intentions.

It's strange, watching the clarity drain from their minds, sip by sip, as the cocktails tighten their grip. Back in Iqaluit, they speak of sobriety with sharp tongues and moral posture—but out here, they don't just drink. They guzzle, reckless and loud. Then begins the spiral: the weepy, self-congratulatory or self-pitying monologues, echoing through my hull like water rushing through loosened boards.

If you've ever stood on a wooden boat that shuddered without warning, you might think the captain was correcting to the current. But no. That's the boat. That's what it feels like when a vessel flinches—when something foul passes through and we cannot bear it.

Most days, I can hold the note in, keep the measure steady.

But on some days, I must respond. Physically.

This hypocrisy was not new to me. As I said, I was born far to the south, in a land where trees still grow. For years, I did just that—growing slowly, reaching incrementally toward the sun with each passing season. I learned in fragments, from those who rested beneath me or leaned their weary backs against my trunk. Sometimes it was a cheek, a hand, a sleeping body curled into my roots—and that was enough. Through touch, I could slip quietly into their dreams, listening to the subtle music of their inner worlds.

In time, I grew older. Wiser, perhaps—but with that wisdom came sorrow, and a quiet disillusionment. Not with those who came to rest in my shade, but with the ones who made them run. From their stories, I learned of lands far beyond the one where my roots took hold. Of rulers cloaked in titles and flags, seated behind distant desks, making choices that tore people from their homes and scattered them into unfamiliar forests like mine, forests where great harm unfolded beneath their branches.

It seemed to me that humans were just as quick to wound as they were to embrace. Neighbours turning on neighbours, often without warning. Faith—something that, for some, once offered solace—twisted again and again into a blade of justification. Genocide after genocide, belief sharpened into cruelty.

The same hands that penned lullabies or coaxed music from strings could also craft devices that shattered bodies in a breath. I watched. I listened. And the longer I did, the less I understood.

The adults who leaned against me never answered my questions.

And the children—I left them be. Let them remain what they were: young, unburdened, untouched by the weight I had come to hold within.

GUESTS

I sensed the same confusion in the captain. Like me, he was repulsed by the men aboard his boat, but necessity is cruel—and he needed the money. He spoke one thing and thought another, his words rowing in one direction while his heart drifted elsewhere. In that, he was no different from the men who paid for his time. But it wasn't in his nature, and I could feel how it tore at him.

They pretended to care—about his past, his family, his language. They ask questions, nod politely. But in their minds, they had already consigned him—and his whole community—to oblivion. His stories were scratched lightly into the ice of their minds and were destined to melt away.

Whenever we depart, the algae and biofilm clinging to my hull always ask the same thing: *Is this the day?* The day I run myself aground on purpose, or split open on a rock in the shallows—just to drift out to deeper water and disappear beneath the surface. They're not the brightest organisms, and never seem to remember: I have no say in where I go or how fast. I move as I'm commanded. I listen.

That isn't to say those who live on my hull are simple, or incapable of learning. In time, they begin to absorb what I've gathered from others—ideas about numbers, rhythms, the way power forgets the uniqueness of every living thing. We've had intimate conversations, even grown close. But just when they begin to grasp the harder truths, I feel the water lower, the winch tighten, the scrape of metal along my sides. I know then: their time with me is over.

They're scrubbed away—minds and all. And I'm lowered again, clean, into the current where it all begins anew. The same questions. The same naïve hope.

Now and then, a barnacle or two clings on. They don't ask much. Mostly, they complain about the cold, muttering endlessly about the tide and when it will finally go out so they can return to the muck.

I've heard people speak that way—about colleagues, or family they can't stand but still must face. That's what barnacles are like to me. There's nothing to learn from them—only how cold they are.

And so, one of the silences I truly love is this: the void that follows when a barnacle is scraped away, and their shrillness finally fades.

MEN

The first hand that touches me belongs to one of the worst. Like all the men here—except the captain—he's from the south. He looks around more than the others, says how beautiful the land is. But inside, he's already imagining how it can be carved into something that fits him.

Years ago, a student on the boat told me about a creature called the zombie spider. It's a spider bitten by a moth; as the larvae grow, they release a chemical—a hallucinogen—that forces the spider to change its web. Not for itself, but for them. To hold them, feed them, protect them—even as they devour it from within.

That's what this man is to me. A moth trying to devour the fabric of this place. He stares at the land and the ocean and tries—desperately—to plant his vision into the heart of the community. A vision that will consume it, strand by strand, from the inside out.

THE BOAT

A little egg here. A little egg there. He'll wait. He'll watch. And in time, the very things that once held this place together will be twisted to serve him—his ambition, his pockets, his distant family, who will never know the name of this bay or set foot on its shore. He wants to alter the landscape. Strip out what holds the ridges in place. Tear away the roots that feed the plants.

The second man rises and stands at the stern, watching Iqaluit shrink as we slip past Apex. He was only here for the grocery store. They're expanding it—to squeeze a little more profit from every shelf. With these men, it's always money. Always margins.

But this one is different. I haven't heard a single thought about the land. He's still puzzling over how to keep charging outrageous prices for the simplest things. If he'd been born a century earlier, he might've made a fine snake-oil salesman—slick, smiling, unbothered. At one point, he muttered to the captain about forgetting his sunglasses—said it made it harder to spot belugas and that he was getting a headache. But the headache wasn't from the sun. It was from squinting and scheming, trying to figure out how to bump the price of a can of beans by another dollar. Ten wasn't enough.

Just feed them cheap cake and candy, he thought. *No one will notice.*

This one makes me miss the barnacles.

I'm not quite sure what to make of the third man. He's quieter than the others, but his mind is a storm. He keeps repeating it—six years, six years, only six years—and each time, the words land with a weight I can't quite place. Is it grief? Relief? Joy?

There's something buried in him. Of all the men on this boat, he is the least honest. The others wear their hypocrisy like jackets—visible, interchangeable, easily shrugged on and off. But him—he tucks his truths beneath the skin, beneath some kind of armour I can't read.

He asks the captain three times more questions than anyone else, but never really listens. He's an actor, used to standing above the ones he addresses. He performs awe—pretends to marvel at how the captain and his family endure the cold. But in his mind, the play always ends the same: *God be praised.*

Today, though, it's the number six—circling like a gull that refuses to land.

When I slowed near a ringed seal, its body corkscrewing into the depths, his thoughts turned not to wonder, but to burial. How to bury the six.

He believes, somehow, that it's easier to bury things—numbers, memories, sins—in northern communities. As if distance were a kind of absolution.

One of the others had joked about him being baptized by the spray off the side of the boat. He turned, smiled—and thought: *Ye serpents, ye generation of vipers, how can ye escape the damnation of hell?*

I don't know what it means. But I don't like the way it sounds. The old cadence of it. The repetition. The weight behind the words.

And I hope he knows—he'll be joining them.

The fourth man is the youngest. I don't know his exact age, but he's certainly much younger than the others. There's more light in him—more optimism—but I can already feel it cracking, like spring ice beneath a warming wind.

I forget the name of the painting, but a few years ago, a woman stood on my deck, speaking of a trip to Europe. There was a painting she loved. She said its meaning shifted depending on the viewer—their mood, their angle, the quality of the light, even how long they stood before it. She'd gone with six others and each of them saw something different. One saw grief, another pain. One called it unfinished. Another called it juvenile. The painting never changed, but people did, and that changed everything. I think this man is like that painting. You could stand before him for hours and still not be sure what you're looking at. Some might see kindness in him. Others might see ambition. Some days, I think he doesn't even know what's beneath the surface—or maybe he does, and he's just learned how to stay still enough not to be read.

His thoughts aren't with his students. Not with the community. Not with the land we're passing by.

Today, all he's thinking about is what he'll buy in Toronto, as he weighs how much longer the salary can keep him tethered to a place he quietly resents.

Like the others, he loves the money. He likes the simplicity—the rhythm of repetition, the absence of real scrutiny. Sadly, most southerners who come north do. They enjoy the freedom that comes with distance. Their managers and head offices are far away—too far to hear what's whispered, or what's ignored.

More time off. More unmonitored sick days. More mental health days, while the children under their care board buses at -40°.

So that is my cargo. Four visitors.

We'll head out to an island tonight. While they drink, sing, and pass out, I'll wait in the water and speak with those who visit me. That's the beauty of this time of year—as the ice breaks, new paths open for the wildlife to travel.

NIGHT

The water around me is quiet—the kind of quiet that settles when the tide evens out and the wind lies low across the bay. I'm tethered to the island now, a thick rope stretching from my bow to a ring of stone where the men dragged it ashore. They haven't gone far—just over the low ridge where the rocks break the wind.

I can still hear them, their laughter rising in bursts, a bottle passed between hands shaky from travel and yesterday's abandon. I wait in the shallows, anchored in silence.

NOT THE SAME ROAD OUT

That's when I feel it—a shift in the current, then the smooth rise of breath from below.

The beluga comes slow, cautious, pale as bone beneath the dark water. It circles once, brushing the edge of my hull. A ringed seal surfaces nearby, slick and alert, its eyes catching the moonlight. They speak in sound—clicks and pulses stitched into the skin of the sea. I listen, as I always do, when they press their heads against me.

"You swam near the cruise ship again?" the seal asks.

The beluga clicks low, sorrow threading its tone. "Too close. It loomed into the sky—lights in every window, engines growling in the ocean's soul."

The seal exhales, shifting. "I swam under one last season. Trash fluttered in its wake like kelp."

The beluga glides along my side. "Warm water trails behind them. The wrong kind of warm. Its colours sting."

The seal drifts toward my stern, quiet for a while. "They'll keep coming. They think this place is pristine and unspoiled."

The beluga clicks again, softer now. "Where can we hide if they keep coming?"

I feel them drift away, their shapes fading into the dark. I creak softly in the cold, the rope stretched taut against the land.

The men will return when the bottle's dry—and when they, too, want to be emptied.

For reasons I've never fully understood, they'd rather wade into the freezing ocean than walk across solid ground.

And every time they do, they reach for me. They grip my side like I'm steady, like I'm safe.

But in those moments, a darker truth surfaces—one I've come to know too well.

Drunkards think in raw, unfiltered bursts. The thoughts may slur, may swell with exaggeration, but buried beneath the noise is something real. Something sharp.

I've heard them confess what no sober light could coax out—regrets soured into anger, tenderness twisted into shame.

Sadness can lead to love. But love, left too long in the cold, curdles into regret.

And regret, in their mouths, often flares into rage.

When the drink takes hold, they're lost inside themselves—trapped in a behavioural maze. Turning, retreating, lashing out at everything and nothing.

I've never seen one make it out.

If they had, they wouldn't keep stumbling back into the maze, night after night, searching for something they've already broken.

MOON

It's calm now, and it must be late. No one has come down to hold my side, so they must be sleeping. These are the hours I feel most alone—adrift but unmoving, tethered but unnoticed. It's in moments like this I wish I could see.

I've heard so much about the moon. They speak of it often—its light, its pull, its presence. I wonder if it's out now. If the sky is clear and the moon hangs high, reflected across the water like a great, watching eye on the back of a whale about to breach.

If only I could see who I carry.

I'm tired of relying on what they say—or more often, what they hide. I have no idea what the truth is—only fragments, spoken or muttered or cried out in weakness. I don't know who they really are beneath the weight of their stories. But if I were given just one moment with the moon—just a glimpse, enough to see it clearly, and then see it reflected in the water—I think I might understand more. To witness the real thing and its echo, side by side. That would be clarity.

Instead, all I have is the reflection. Altered by breeze, shifted by every ripple and swell. It's not the moon itself—only a suggestion, a flicker. And when alcohol and exhaustion return tomorrow, I'll be left again with only distortions, the moon's image broken across the surface.

Clarity. Where is mine to come from, if all I learn comes from the odd and the flawed, boarding me day after day?

THOUGHT

Maybe there's no such thing as pure clarity. Maybe we all just shift a little, one way or another, the way I drift across the bay—always leaning toward the Labrador Sea, though I'll never reach it.

The only absolute is this: a beginning, and an end. Everything in between is just wandering—if you're given the luxury of wandering—and wondering where the end lies, and why the beginning ever mattered.

CLARITY

But there are rare moments when even the worst of my cargo merges, briefly, with the good.

At night, when we anchor in the bay and they all look up, they stare in awe. It's one of the few times I've felt people truly at peace. Their goodness or badness doesn't vanish—it's simply silenced by something greater.

A single dot, a solitary blade of grass tipped with light, grows into a field, then a forest, then a neon flame spilling across the sky—only to vanish again. No moment of the aurora borealis is ever the same.

Maybe that's why they feel at peace. They're witnessing something that belongs only to them. For once, they might feel special.

I've carried poets, singers, painters, philosophers, sculptors, scientists. Not one has claimed a poem, a painting, or an equation that could match the beauty of this release of energy.

Maybe there's no such thing as perfect clarity. But there must be moments of it—fleeting, like the lights above.

MAUDLIN

Why did I have to be cut down?

CAPTAIN

I'm not going to write about the captain. I respect him too much. It was his singing that taught me my love of music I cannot hear—but I can feel his mind shift, and the words linger and cascade. He, his family, his community—they don't need me to speak on their behalf.

SILENCE

I lied before. I said the moon was enough—but it never was. The moon belongs to everyone, doesn't it? It hangs above every rooftop, every open sea. And those who board me always marvel at the northern lights, as if wonder could absolve their cruelty, as if beauty alone could make them kind. No. I need more than hallowed light. I crave what's rare here—silence. I ache for stillness, the kind that settles deep, like wind-packed snow.

I'll strike a rock near the pier—cleanly, deliberately. The tide will be low. Their walk home will be easy. I'll be a wreck with a bruise, not a break, a gesture more than a scream.

"But you might die," whispered the mussel.

No. I just need time alone. That's what's rare here—time untouched, unshared. They'll leave, and in a week they'll return with ropes and tools, ready to reclaim and cleanse me.

"Then why go through it all?" the mussel asked.

Because sometimes there is such beauty.

But I am so tired.

So bloody tired.

The boat turned. The mussel closed.

Contributors

Lillian Au is a writer and broadcast journalist from North Vancouver, British Columbia. Her non-fiction story, "Arviat" was featured in the anthology, *Upon a Midnight Clear* (Tidewater Press, 2024). Her poetry and memoir work have appeared in *Ricepaper Magazine* and been recognized by the International Amy MacRae Award for Memoir and the Chinese Canadian Museum.

Anne Baldo's short fiction has appeared in a number of publications, including *Broken Pencil*, *Carousel Magazine*, *Hermine*, *Qwerty* and *SubTerrain*. Her creative nonfiction piece, "Expecting," was longlisted for the 2019 CBC Nonfiction Prize. *Morse Code for Romantics* (Porcupine's Quill, 2023) is her first collection; her novel, *One Day, Hard and Clear*, is forthcoming with Dundurn Press. She lives in Windsor, Ontario.

Bill Engleson is a retired social worker, pickleball aficionado, energetic novelist, poet, humourist, essayist, and flash fictionista. He is the author of two novels (*The Life of Gronsky* and *Like a Child to Home*) and a collection of humorous literary essays, *Confessions of an Inadvertently Gentrifying Soul*. He is an engaged community volunteer who lives on Denman Island, BC.

Matthew Heneghan is an author, public speaker, and mental health advocate based in Falkland, BC. A former military and civilian paramedic, he was diagnosed with PTSD shortly before the tragic loss of his mother to suicide in 2017. Matthew is the author of the

CONTRIBUTORS

memoir, *A Medic's Mind*, and *Woven in War*, a tribute to military sacrifice now archived at the Canadian War Museum. His work has been featured by CBC, CTV, and in several anthologies, earning national recognition, including the British Columbia Medal of Good Citizenship.

dee Hobsbawn-Smith is an award-winning author, essayist, poet, fictionist, chef, curious cook, food writer, and runner who lives rurally west of Saskatoon, Saskatchewan. An ex-restaurateur and longtime freelance journalist, she has written ten books, including *Bread & Water: essays* (University of Regina Press, 2021), winner of the SK Book Awards Nonfiction Award, the gold medal for culinary narrative from Taste Canada, and is the SK Libraries Association's 2025 selection for One Book One Province. Her most recent book is *Among the Untamed* (Frontenac House, 2023), winner of the 2024 SK Book Awards Poetry Award.

Sharon Hunt's short stories have appeared in Canadian literary magazines such as *The Antigonish Review*; other stories are forthcoming in anthologies. Her first mystery story, published in *Ellery Queen Mystery Magazine*, was shortlisted for two international awards, while one, in *Alfred Hitchcock Mystery Magazine*, was selected for inclusion in *The Best American Mystery Stories, 2019*. Currently, she is working on a collection of stories about loss and remembrance.

Tracy Kreuzburg is currently a student of the Creative Writing Diploma program at Memorial University, Newfoundland. She has a background in social work, including addiction counselling and working with Afghan refugees. Her stories have appeared in anthologies and she has also had poetry published. Her tale, "The Corpse Washers," won first place in WritersNL's annual "A Nightmare on George Street" in 2023. Tracy lives in Corner Brook, Newfoundland

and Labrador, located within the traditional territories of the Mi'kmaq people, specifically the area known as Elmastukwek.

Seyward Goodhand's stories have been shortlisted for the Writers' Trust/McClelland & Stewart Journey Prize and a National Magazine Award and longlisted for the CBC Short Story Prize. Her first book, *Even That Wildest Hope* (Invisible Publishing, 2019), was a finalist for the Manitoba Book Awards' Margaret Laurence Award for Fiction and the Eileen McTavish Sykes Award for Best First Book, and longlisted for the 2020 Sunburst Award for Excellence in Canadian Literature of the Fantastic. Seyward lives in Winnipeg, Manitoba.

Lauren LaFrance is a graduate in Biology and Psychology and has recently completed a creative writing course at the University of Prince Edward Island. While she has read her fiction and poetry at local events and open mics, "Kick-Ass" is her first published work. Lauren lives on the North Shore, Prince Edward Island.

Tricia Snell is a writer and flutist, author of fiction, poetry and non-fiction. Her story, "Out to the Horses," was longlisted for the 2019 CBC Short Story Award and published in *Room* magazine (Dec 2019), while the story "A Glass of Vodka" was included in the PEN Syndicated Fiction Project /National Public Radio show, *The Sound of Writing*. Her writing has appeared in *Every Day Fiction*, *Art Papers*, *Oregon Humanities*, *The Oregonian*, and *The Grove Review*. Tricia lives in Lunenburg, Nova Scotia.

Karen Solie was born in Moose Jaw and grew up in southwest Saskatchewan. Her seventh collection of poems, *Wellwater*, was published in 2025 in Canada by Anansi, in the UK by Picador, and is forthcoming in the US from Farrar, Straus, & Giroux in 2026. Poems from the collection have been published in Canada, the US,

CONTRIBUTORS

UK, Europe, Ireland, and Australia, and are included in *The Best Canadian Poetry* 2025 and *The Best American Poetry* 2024. She is a half-time lecturer in creative writing at the University of St Andrews in Scotland.

Bev Vincent is the author of several non-fiction books, including *The Road to the Dark Tower* and *Stephen King: A Complete Exploration of His Work, Life, and Influences*. In 2018, he co-edited the anthology *Flight or Fright* with Stephen King and has published nearly 150 stories since 2000, with appearances in magazines like *Cemetery Dance* and *Ellery Queen's*, *Alfred Hitchcock's* and *Black Cat Mystery Magazines*. His work has been published in over 20 languages and nominated for the Stoker (twice), Edgar, Ignotus, Locus, Rondo Hatton Classic Horror and ITW Thriller Awards. Originally from New Brunswick, he now lives in Texas with his wife.

Terry Watada is a well-published author with four novels, six poetry books, and a short story collection in print. His most recent novel, *Hiroshima Bomb Money* (NeWest Press 2024), is the culmination of his exploration of the Japanese and Japanese Canadian experience. Living in Toronto, Terry is also a musician and recording artist.

Patrick Woodcock is the author of ten poetry collections and numerous reviews, with his work translated into fourteen languages. His seventh book, *Always Die Before Your Mother* (ECW Press, 2009), was shortlisted for the ReLit Award and reached number one on *The Globe and Mail*'s bestseller list. *You Can't Bury Them All* (ECW Press, 2016) was a finalist for the JM Abraham Poetry Award. His latest release is *Farhang Book One* (ECW Press, 2023), with *Farhang Book Two* forthcoming in Fall 2026. He currently serves as the Regional Instructor Coordinator for Nunavut with United for Literacy.